GIRL OF THE YEAR™ 2017

Gabriela

Speaks Out

American Girl®

GIRL OF THE YEAR™ 2017

Gabriela Speaks Out

by Teresa E. Harris

Scholastic Inc.

Published by Scholastic Inc., *Publishers since 1920.* SCHOLASTIC and associated logos are trademarks and/or registered trademarks of Scholastic Inc.

Book design by Angela Jun
Cover photos: girl: Michael Frost for Scholastic; lock © john500/Getty Images; lockers: © H. Mark Weidman Photography/Alamy Stock Photo
Cover photo retouched by Carol Tessitore

ISBN 978-1-338-13700-2
10 9 8 7 6 5 4 3 2 1   17 18 19 20 21

Printed in the U.S.A. 58 • First printing 2017

SCHOLASTIC

For Keith

— T.H.

Contents

Forever Friends

Chapter 1

"Okay," my best friend, Teagan Harmon, said. "One word that describes this summer. Go!"

"Just one word?"

Teagan nodded, a sly smile spreading across her freckled face. The two of us were over at Teagan's house, sprawled across her back lawn. I was full to bursting with Teagan's grandfather's one-of-a-kind raspberry lemonade and top-secret-recipe chicken salad. The day couldn't have been more . . .

"Perfect!" I declared, barely able to contain the word inside me.

Teagan sat up and pulled her strawberry-blonde hair away from her neck. Normally, Teagan wore her favorite turquoise beanie, no matter the weather. But the end-of-August heat was too much even for her. Mr. Harmon,

Teagan's grandfather, had called the heat "downright oppressive. The kind of weather that makes you too hot to do anything, even think."

Not for me, though. I couldn't stop my mind from replaying the events of the summer over and over like they were scenes from a movie. And I couldn't stop hitting rewind.

In my head I saw Liberty Arts Center, my favorite place in the world, an old brick building that sat right smack in the middle of Germantown Avenue. Mama, the director of Liberty, called the center the jewel in the crown of the surrounding community. And she was right—the community depended on Liberty for art and dance classes, poetry, too, and our yearly Rhythm and Views show that featured it all. But just that summer, Liberty had suffered a massive electrical failure that threatened to close the center for good. It took the whole Liberty family coming together—dancers, poets, and artists—to raise money for the repairs. We did a viral video, rallies, and my most favorite event of the summer by far—a performance in the park that I'd choreographed. The thought of it put a smile on my face to rival the August sun. The August sun that would soon turn into September, which meant . . .

"Now, what's one word you'd use to describe starting

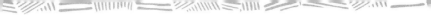

middle school?" We'd be starting sixth grade at Kelly Middle School in just two weeks' time.

"Huh? Oh, um . . ." Teagan blinked rapidly, as though I'd just snapped her out of her own thoughts. "Um," she said again.

"Let me help you out. Mega-crazy-exciting!"

Teagan gave me a look.

"That is totally one word," I said, "and I'm sticking to it. What about you?"

Teagan lay down beside me and then sat up quickly again. She tied her hair up into a ponytail, then reached for her coding notebook, which she'd nicknamed Cody. She began flipping mindlessly through its pages.

Teagan was a lot of things. A problem-solver. A genius (though she didn't like when people called her that). What she wasn't was the kind of person who was ever at a loss for words, much less a single one.

"Exciting is a good word," she said softly. "And perfect is a good word for this summer."

"Of course!" I shouted, propping myself up on my elbow. "We saved Liberty, *and* put on an awesome show with awesome dancing and equally amazing poetry, courtesy of . . ." I cleared my throat dramatically and made a show of pointing from Teagan to me.

She managed a weak smile that was nothing like the sly, playful grin she'd flashed at me only moments before. The last time I could remember seeing that look on her face was last month, when we'd gotten into our first-ever argument about the way Teagan used to jump in and talk for me all the time when I stuttered. I didn't like seeing that look on Teagan's face then, and I liked it even less now.

"Wh-What's wrong?" I asked, my nerves—and my stutter—getting the best of me.

Teagan looked away from me. "I'mnotgoingtoKelly." Her words came racing out of her in one breath.

"What?"

Teagan looked down at Cody and started flipping through it again. Pages filled from top to bottom with letters, numbers, and symbols flashed by. "I'm not going to Kelly," Teagan said, more slowly this time.

"What?!" I said again, but I'd heard her loud and clear. I had chosen "excited" for my one word, but if I had to pick a second it would be a word I'd learned last year: "foreboding." School wasn't like Liberty for me—it wasn't a second home where I could speak through dance, the language I spoke best. It was the place where my stutter got in the way so often that some days I hardly spoke at all. Unless Teagan was there, and now she wouldn't be.

"B-B-But wh-why?" I asked. "Wh-Where are y-y-you going to g-g-go? Wh-What a-about about—" Sadness and confusion welled up inside me and I struggled to get my words out. There was a time when Teagan would've filled them in for me, but now she waited patiently. This made me feel even worse. Sometimes kids at school made fun of me when I stuttered, especially this one girl, Aaliyah Reade-Johnson. But never Teagan. A hole opened up inside me, too big to fill with all the words in the world.

"I'm going to Main Line Tech," Teagan said, her voice quavering. "My grandpa found out about their STEM programs—they're the best in all of Philadelphia. I applied earlier this year, and they put me on a waiting list. I thought—" Teagan reached up to dab at her eyes. "I thought I'd never get off that list, and in a way, I was happy. I wanted to go to Kelly with you, but they called last week and said there was a spot open if I wanted it."

"B-B-B-But why w-would you want it?" I cried, fighting back tears.

"Because they have all these math and science classes, even coding classes, and—oh, Gabby, I'm sorry." Teagan burst into tears.

I couldn't help but join her, and for a few minutes, we sat beneath the cloudless, late-August sky, crying our eyes out.

"Who-Who's g-going to h-h-help me take o-on A-A-Aaliyah when she c-calls me R-R-Repeat?" I asked, sniffling.

"You can take her on all by yourself," Teagan said, wiping her eyes on the back of her arm. Her face was bright red and streaked with tears. "Besides, you'll have Isaiah."

Isaiah Jordan was a boy we'd met just a couple months ago. Obsessed with all things Shakespeare, he'd been the one to offer the rec room at his father's church as a place to hold Liberty's programs while the center was closed. It wasn't long before he became part of our poetry group and one of our good friends. This would be his first year in public school—he'd gone to private school up until fifth grade. So, I did have Isaiah. And my cousin Red and Bria and Alejandro, the rest of the poetry group, even though they'd be in seventh grade. But it just wouldn't be the same without Teagan. I felt a fresh wave of tears coming.

"Gabby?" Teagan said. "We're still going to be best friends. Nothing will change. I promise." She reached over and squeezed my hand.

"You r-really pr-pr-promise?" I asked.

Teagan nodded. I squeezed her hand back. Teagan jumped suddenly, as though an idea had just occurred to her. She pulled a pencil from Cody's spiral spine, opened to a clean page in the back of Cody, and at the top of the page she wrote Forever Friends. Then she held the eraser to her chin, thinking, before she began to write.

Forever friends through thicker and thinner

She handed me the notebook and pencil.

"You-You are wr-writing a poem in-in C-Cody?" I flipped the notebook closed and pointed at the cover, where Teagan had written: Cody Harmon, Property of Teagan Harmon. Sole Purpose: Coding. And then, in all capital letters: AND ONLY CODING.

"I take Cody with me everywhere," Teagan said. "I want to take this poem with me everywhere, too." She reached over and flipped Cody back to the poem.

Beneath Teagan's line I wrote:

Through blackouts, rallies, and a girl named Aaliyah

Teagan giggled as she read what I'd written. She nodded for me to continue, so I wrote another line and then handed the notebook back to her. By the time Mr. Harmon came to the patio door and called, "Gabby, your mom is here!" we'd filled up almost the whole page.

Forever friends, through thicker and thinner
Through blackouts, rallies, and a girl named Aaliyah
Through my bumpy speech

And my non-dancing feet
Even though I can't speak a lick of code
And I speak HTML, Java, and Go
I have your back, your front, and all your sides
Main Line Tech or Kelly
We'll stay best friends
For real
Bona fide

Big School, Big Day

Chapter 2

"Ready, Gabby?" Mama called upstairs.

I was as ready as I was ever going to be. My hair was done in a neat, bouncy ponytail, courtesy of Mama. I had on a brand-new outfit still creased from sitting in a shopping bag in the back of my closet, and my book bag, filled to capacity with school supplies, was firmly on my back. In less than an hour, I'd be opening my first-ever locker and changing classes and—

My phone buzzed. A text from Teagan: *Happy first day of school!!!!!!!!!!!!!!* ☺ ☺ ☺ ☺

Happy first day of school to you, too! I wrote back and tried to ignore the pang of sadness in my chest that Teagan wouldn't be with me.

And remember—only an 8% chance! she replied.

Last week, when I asked Teagan what I was supposed to do when Aaliyah Reade-Johnson made fun of me, Teagan went right into Teagan Problem-Solving Mode. She opened the calculator app on her phone and did a lot of complicated math to figure out the chances of me having any classes with Aaliyah. "Eight percent," she had assured me. "In other words, slim to none."

If I could count on anything in this world to be right, it was Teagan's math. I sent her one last bunch of heart emojis, slipped my phone into my backpack, then turned to my gray-and-white cat, Maya, who was curled up in the fuzzy chair beneath my loft bed. "I'm officially in middle school, Maya. Wish me luck!" But Maya just rolled over onto her back, eyes still closed, and purred. Unlike Maya Angelou, the poet I'd named Maya after, my cat did not have a way with words.

I turned off my bedroom light and went downstairs, where I found Mama, Daddy, and my older cousin Red waiting for me by the front door.

"I thought we were going to have to hit Control F to find you," Daddy said, smiling.

Mama always said Daddy's job as a network engineer made him see the whole world as one big computer. He and

Mama were just as excited about me starting middle school as I was—maybe a teensy bit more—and both were going to drop Red and me off.

"This is a big day," Daddy said as we followed Mama out the front door.

"It *is* a big day," she agreed. She'd even swapped out her usual dance teacher uniform of a leotard, yoga pants, and a long cardigan for a silky blouse and some sharp black slacks.

Even though I couldn't wait to be a middle schooler, I really wished Mama and Daddy would stop using the word "big." Big just reminded me how many classes I'd be in without Teagan. About how big a deal my stutter seemed when teachers called on me in class. Some tiny tap dancers started tapping in my belly. I clamped my hand over my stomach to stop them.

"Don't worry, Gabby," Mama said, smiling, as she opened the car door. "We'll get that tummy filled. We're stopping for bagels on the way."

I took a deep breath and slid into the backseat beside Red, who flashed me his toothiest, chipped-tooth grin. Red had been staying with Mama, Daddy, and me for the past six months while his mother, Mama's sister and a doctor in the military, was overseas on what Red called "a tour."

Before he put on his seat belt, Red leaned over to me and whispered, "It *is* a big day, cuz. You won't forget it. Just wait and see. It's gonna be awesome." He wriggled his eyebrows.

There it was, the word "big" again. The more Mama, Daddy, and Red said it, the more those three letters started to feel like they were looming over me, casting shadows everywhere.

"I should tell you, though," said Red, lowering his voice, "there are a few things incoming sixth graders need to know."

"L-Like what?"

"Like the fact that all of your classes are in the basement, and most of the rooms down there are filled with mold. Oh, and they serve you leftovers for lunch."

I stared at Red. Leftovers? Classes in the basement? Mold? The tippity-tapping in my stomach picked up pace.

"You c-can't be sssserious!" A vision of Isaiah and me sitting down to a lunch of bread crusts and half-empty containers of apple juice flashed through my mind. "Th-Th-That's not even l-legal!" I shouted.

Red's smile dimmed a bit.

"Everything all right back there?" Daddy called, glancing in the rearview mirror.

"Everything's fine, Uncle Rob," Red said quickly. Then, to me, "Calm down, cuz. I'm just messing with you. Your classes aren't in the basement and there's no mold anywhere in the building, at least so far as I know. And they can't serve you leftovers." He flashed me his chipped-tooth grin again. "Middle school is awesome. Just you wait and see."

But what if it wasn't awesome? What if I had mean teachers? What if I couldn't get my locker open? The what-ifs piled up all around me, so many that a bagel with butter and jelly from my favorite deli couldn't even take my mind off of them.

By the time we pulled up to Kelly and spilled out of the car, I wasn't so sure I was ready for middle school. At all.

The tiny tap dancers started up in my stomach again, and this time I was sure they'd brought five friends apiece.

Speaking of friends, Red couldn't wait to find his. No sooner did his feet hit the sidewalk than he took off, calling, "See you later, cuz, Aunt Tina, Uncle Rob."

"Not so fast, Clifford," Mama called after him.

Red came reluctantly back, his hands shoved into the pockets of his khaki cargo shorts.

"A picture for your mom first?" Mama asked, opening the camera app on her phone.

Red obliged, sticking his tongue out at the last second.

"I think that'll do it," Mama said, laughing and shaking her head.

He slapped me gently on the shoulder. "Good luck today, cuz." He wriggled his eyebrows. Then he turned to Mama. "Before I go. Aunt Tina, maybe you can ease up on that Clifford stuff around here? I've got a reputation to maintain."

Mama laughed again and Daddy joined in and for a moment my nerves settled down. But seconds later, Red was gone and my insides started to jitterbug again. I looked up to find Mama and Daddy staring down at me, concern etched across their faces.

"Are you all right, Gabby?" Daddy asked.

"I-I. I just-just—" I stopped. Mama and Daddy waited patiently while I found my words. "I-I'm j-j-just scared," I said at last. And before I knew it, there were a million more what-ifs in my head.

What if I didn't make any new friends?

What if I didn't have any classes with Isaiah? The Jordans had just gotten back from their vacation yesterday, so I hadn't had a chance to check with Isaiah.

"Oh, Gabby, you'll make plenty of friends," Mama said,

doing that thing where she practically reads my mind. "Do you know why? Because you're smart. You're caring, and you're talented and brave. Just think of all of the stuff you did this summer to save Liberty."

"And if people make fun of you for stuttering, ignore them and keep right on talking," Daddy said. "Just like Mrs. Baxter always tells you."

Mrs. Baxter was the district speech therapist. I'd been working with her since second grade, and she must have told me a million times already to ignore people who made fun of me. But sometimes, it was easier said than done, *especially* if one of those people was Aaliyah Reade-Johnson.

"And why don't we just ask Isaiah if he has any of the same classes as you?" Mama said, looking over my shoulder.

Isaiah and his parents were climbing out of a sleek black Cadillac. Today, Isaiah wore his favorite *Prose Before Bros* T-shirt while Mr. Jordan, who was the tallest man I'd ever met, wore his usual three-piece suit and shiny-as-a-new-penny shoes. Isaiah's mom was almost the complete opposite of his dad, short, squat, and dressed down in a pair of jeans and a T-shirt. Daddy waved the two of them over, and while he and Mama chatted with Isaiah's parents, I compared schedules with Isaiah.

"We have math and lunch together!" I said.

"'As good luck would have it'!" Isaiah declared, and I couldn't help but laugh. Isaiah was here with me, spouting Shakespeare lines, *and* we had math and lunch together. The tiny tap dancers slowed down a bit and then a bit more.

The bell rang.

Mama and Daddy grabbed me for one last hug. Mr. Jordan squeezed Isaiah's shoulder. His mother planted a big, sloppy kiss on his forehead.

"You remember what we talked about, right?" Mrs. Jordan asked.

Isaiah nodded. With another shoulder clap and a second kiss, Mr. and Mrs. Jordan were gone.

Mama herded Isaiah and me together for a photo and then said, "You two are going to be fine, right?"

"'There is nothing either good or bad, but thinking makes it so,'" Isaiah replied.

"Okay. Right. That's good, Isaiah," Mama replied, looking slightly confused. She turned to me. "Gabby?"

I took a deep breath, faced Kelly, and pointed at Isaiah. "What he said."

Mama and Daddy laughed. With one more wave they were gone, and Isaiah and I began making our way to Kelly's front door.

"Let's rock this," I said, echoing what Mama sometimes said before I went onstage for a dance performance at Liberty.

This time Isaiah pointed at me. "What you said."

Egg Salad and Enemies

Chapter 3

Okay, so it turned out Red's teasing really was just teasing. So far, sixth grade was actually completely awesome. For the first time ever, I had a locker. The sixth-grade teachers had designed laminated name tags and taped them to the front. My name tag was written in purpley pink, my favorite color. And none of my classes in the morning, including my homeroom, were in the basement. In fact, they were in Kelly's newer wing, with hallway after hallway covered in bright bulletin boards with signs that read things like WELCOME, SIXTH GRADERS! and YOUR JOURNEY BEGINS NOW!

But even better than a locker and the new wing? I hadn't seen Aaliyah Reade-Johnson once.

By the time lunch rolled around, the tiny tap dancers from this morning had taken their bow.

Egg Salad and Enemies

Isaiah and I met just outside the cafeteria, like we'd planned. I beamed at him. He managed a smile back, but there was something else mixed in. I couldn't quite figure out what.

"So I'll get my lunch while you find us a table?" I asked as we headed into the cafeteria.

When we first met Isaiah this summer, he'd whipped out the most pristine lunch I'd ever seen: perfectly packed snacks, juice in a thermos, and a cheese sandwich shaped like a star. I didn't expect any less from him for our first day of school.

"Actually," he said, following me to the lunch line, "I'm branching out." He made a lackluster gesture toward the cafeteria food in front of us.

I raised an eyebrow at him. Who voluntarily branched out from star-shaped sandwiches to cold tater tots and soggy egg salad sandwiches?

Isaiah placed a sandwich on his tray. "It's what my mom was talking about when she was all, 'Remember what we talked about?' They say I get too fixated on things. Like never eating school lunch . . ."

He took a helping of corn and made a face. I did the same. This wasn't leftovers like Red had said, but it wasn't fine dining, either.

"They say they're not trying to torture me or anything, but they feel like I should try different stuff once in a while." The look on Isaiah's face suggested that he thought his parents most certainly *were* trying to torture him. Or maybe he just didn't like corn.

We quickly paid and found our way to a table in the corner. Once seated, Isaiah reached into his backpack and pulled out a book titled *In the Name of Justice: Voices of Black Activist Poets.*

"That looks like a cool book," I said. "Red told me all about how black people used their words to fight injustices during the Harlem Renaissance and civil rights movement."

If there was one thing Red knew, it was poetry, or, as he called it, "laying down rhymes" or "versin' and vibin'." And when he'd first come to stay with us, he'd wasted no time in spreading his love of versin' and vibin' by forming a poetry group at Liberty. At first it had just been Red, Teagan, and me, but it wasn't long before the group recruited two more seventh graders, Bria and Alejandro, and eventually Isaiah.

"Yeah, my parents told me the same thing about the civil rights movement when they gave me this book," Isaiah said, staring down at the cover. "They want me to read more widely, learn about new things. Because, well, they think

I'm a bit obsessed with Shakespeare." He placed the book down on the table and then took a tentative bite of his sandwich.

Isaiah *was* more than a bit obsessed with Shakespeare, but I wasn't about to tell him that, not when he hadn't even tasted the tater tots yet.

"Well, I think branching out is a great idea," I said, dunking a tot in ketchup. "Expand our horizons and all that, like Mr. Harmon always says."

The mention of Mr. Harmon made me suddenly aware of how Teagan wasn't here eating lunch with us. I wondered what lunch at Main Line Tech was like. I imagined Teagan sitting across from some kid with big glasses talking about protons and HTML or whatever else geniuses study. And the important question: Were her tater tots as gross as these? I decided to text her right after school to find out.

"You all right, Gabby?" Isaiah asked.

I nodded, but the thought of Teagan had made me feel heavy, like I was carrying half a dozen dance bags filled with tap shoes made of cement. I didn't want anything to ruin my awesome first day, so I changed the subject and said, "Let's come up with a limerick about this yucky food."

At once, Isaiah's face broke into a smile. He wasted no time diving right in. "There once was a school named Kelly.

It served lunch that was really smelly. Watered down corn. Tater tots half-done. I think I'd rather have pork belly."

"Ew!" I cried, collapsing into a fit of giggles.

Isaiah laughed along with me, and I couldn't help thinking that if Teagan couldn't be here, I was sure glad it was Isaiah who was.

After lunch, Isaiah and I had our first math class together. Our teacher, Mr. Newman, stood at the front of the room and droned on and on about the rules and regulations. Whenever he turned to write something on the board, Isaiah and I passed limericks to each other.

"Math is a fundamental area of study, which is why I expect . . ."

As Isaiah scribbled down another poem, my mind drifted back to the Aaliyah math Teagan had done for me last week. An 8 percent chance of having class with Aaliyah. Teagan should've said I had a 0 percent chance of seeing Aaliyah at all, I realized happily. There was one period left in the day and so far, I hadn't laid eyes on her.

The bell rang and it was officially time for the eighth and final period. Social studies with a teacher named Ms.

Tottenham, who was waiting at her classroom door, smiling at us like she'd never been so happy to see a group of people in her life. She had fruit-punch-colored dreadlocks piled on top of her head in a massive bun, and freckles dusted across her smooth brown cheeks. She wore a long dress covered in a design that looked like splotches of paint, and both of her wrists were piled high with bracelets that made a sound like the chime above Liberty's front door whenever she moved her arms.

"Good afternoon, Gabriela," she said as I approached her class.

I stopped in my tracks. "H-How d-do you know m-my name?" I wasn't like Teagan, famous throughout the district for being a whiz.

If possible, Ms. Tottenham's smile grew even wider. "I saw you on the news this summer," she said, talking about the segment that had featured our park performance for Liberty. "You're something of a local celebrity, are you not?"

My face grew hot. A local celebrity? *Me?* "N-Not r-r-really," I mumbled, but I couldn't help but smile a little as a ripple of pride washed over me. I slipped past Ms. Tottenham and into the classroom.

For the second time in less than a minute, I stopped dead in my tracks. My smile melted off my face as my stomach lurched.

Aaliyah Reade-Johnson sat in the front row. Right smack in the middle.

SPLAT!

Chapter 4

At first she didn't see me. She was too busy organizing her supplies on her desk, moving her notebook until it was perfectly centered and then taking her time sticking her pencils neatly in the desk's groove.

An 8 percent chance. I must have jinxed it. I kicked myself inside and wished more than ever that Teagan were standing here beside me. She'd link her arm through mine and together we'd march right by Aaliyah's desk without so much as a backward glance. *But Teagan isn't here,* I reminded myself. I'd have to face Aaliyah all by myself.

That is, of course, if she realized I was here.

Don't let her see you, Gabby, I told myself, and hurried quickly to a desk in the back. But that desk had a name tag on it. So did the rest of the ones in the back row. I looked around for my own name tag. *Don't let my seat be near Aaliyah. Don't let my seat be near Aaliyah.* The chant played over and over again in my head, pounding out a rhythm as rapid as my heart. I didn't find my name tag in the second-to-last row or the third one, either.

At last I spotted it, propped up on the desk behind Aaliyah's. My heart sank even further, this time right into my shoes. Maybe she wouldn't turn around at all for the entire school year and notice me sitting there. I inched slowly toward my desk.

Aaliyah turned around. Our eyes met. For a moment she stared at me blankly and I thought that maybe she'd decided to let go of whatever it was that happened in fifth grade that had made her hate me.

"H-Hi," I said. I pointed awkwardly at my desk. "I-I'm h-here."

"That's nice," Aaliyah said, sounding like she thought it was anything but. She made a big show of looking around. "What happened to your sidekick?"

"Sss-Sidekick?"

Aaliyah rolled her eyes. "Teagan Whatsherface."

I was quite certain Aaliyah knew Teagan's last name, but I just muttered, "M-Main L-Line," and slid into my seat.

She turned back to face the front of the room, just as the

remainder of the class came pouring in. When Zuri Moore and Victoria Thornton realized their assigned seats were on either side of Aaliyah, they sucked their teeth. Zuri muttered, "Perfect. Just perfect," under her breath. If Aaliyah heard this, she didn't let on.

"There's mine!" Josiah Benton cried from the front of the room. He took off at a run, his backpack slamming into Aaliyah's desk on his way and sending her perfectly arranged notebook and pencils flying. There was a collective "Ooooh," and then silence. Victoria snickered.

"Sorry," Josiah mumbled, and then he hurried away so fast you would've thought someone lit a fire beneath the soles of his brand-new sneakers.

Glaring at Josiah, Aaliyah retrieved her belongings, arranged them neatly on her desk again, and then reached up to smooth her always-perfect bun. No matter what—gym, recess, a strong gust of wind—I'd never seen a single strand of Aaliyah's hair out of place. Teagan used to say that was because even Aaliyah's hair was scared of her. Then she'd collapse into a fit of giggles and laugh until her face was beet red. The thought of Teagan's laughing face made a smile spread across mine.

"Something funny, Repeat?"

I looked up to find Aaliyah turned all the way around

in her seat again, glaring at me now, her eyes narrowed beneath her thick, dark brows. I knew that look well.

"Wh-What? I-I-I w-w-wasn't—"

"Good afternoon, boys and girls!" Ms. Tottenham declared as she entered the classroom and closed the door behind her.

Aaliyah turned back around, but not before she got in one last dirty look at me. I sank down as low as I could in my seat, feeling heavier by the second, as Ms. Tottenham spread her bangled arms wide and said, "Welcome!" She beamed at us. "I don't think I've ever seen a lovlier group of faces. I hope you all are ready for sixth grade, which I have always considered the best year ever."

It could've been, I thought. *Until I ended up having social studies with Aaliyah Reade-Johnson.*

"Wait," Isaiah said when we met up outside school to walk home at the end of the day. "You have social studies with, um, Alison Reaves-Jackson?"

"Aaliyah Reade-Johnson," I hissed, and looked around frantically. It would be just my luck for her to think I was laughing at her *and* talking about her, all in the same day.

"And who is she again?" Isaiah asked.

"My mortal enemy," I replied, hiking my backpack higher on my back.

Isaiah's eyes went wide. He stared at me and said, "You're exaggerating, right?"

I shook my head.

"She's the ab-absolute-solute w-worst," I declared, and I told Isaiah all about how Aaliyah had come to our school last year, when fifth grade was already half over, and how there wasn't a day that ended in "y" that Aaliyah wasn't glaring at someone. Okay. Not just any old some-one. Me.

"And you're saying she gave you that nickname because she hates you for no reason?" Isaiah asked.

I nodded. I filled Isaiah in on how, when Aaliyah first arrived, she'd wasted no time talking over the teacher and hogging every class discussion. And that was just her first week. By the end of her third, she'd taken to raising her hand every time the teacher asked a question and answer-ing even if she wasn't called on. Some of the kids in class called her the Know-It-All. Others called her scary.

"And then one day Teagan and I looked up, and she was standing over our lunch table!" I said.

"And?" Isaiah pressed.

"And she said, in this bossy voice, 'I'd like to sit here.' "

"And?" Isaiah again.

Just the thought of it was making my stutter act up. "And then we st-stared at her, because we weren't ex-expecting, I mean . . . I tried-tried to answer her, but I-I kind of st-stuttered and then s-she said, 'Whatever, I didn't want to sit here anyway, Repeat,' and she st-stomped off."

"That's it?" Isaiah asked. "That's why she hates you?"

"Yes."

Isaiah shook his head. "There's nothing scarier than he who hates without reason. Well, in this case, she."

I shuddered. Only an 8 percent chance that I'd have class with She Who Hates Without Reason and it had happened. *And* I had to sit right behind her, too.

"Just ignore her, Gabby," Isaiah said as we came to the end of Kelly Drive and made a left. "Take it from someone who has been made fun of a *lot*. You've just got to look at them and say—" He paused, as though trying to remember something. "'Tried to make me stop laughin', stop lovin', stop livin'—But I don't care! I'm still here!'" At these last words, Isaiah thrust his arms outward like he was trying to hug the world.

I laughed. "That doesn't sound like Shakespeare."

Isaiah dropped his hands back to his sides. "It's not. We did a little independent reading in language arts this afternoon, and I decided to read some of that book my parents gave me."

"So, you're branching out?"

We came to the corner of Magnolia and Lilac. "I'm branching out." Isaiah shrugged. "And the poems are not so bad. Most of them are pretty awesome actually, especially Langston—"

SPLAT!

A water balloon hit Isaiah full in the face, drenching him.

"Wh-What—" I whipped around just in time for another balloon to come soaring over the hedges in front of the library and hit me square in the cheek. Then there was another and another, until Isaiah and I were absolutely soaked. My hair, plastered to my forehead, dripped a stinging combination of water and moisturizer into my eyes. I blinked hard, wiping at my eyes with the hem of my T-shirt, not daring to open them until I'd dried my face as best I could. And when I did, I saw Isaiah standing beside me, his eyes wide with shock, his new poetry book under his arm, now dripping wet. Kids were taking off in all directions, some of them running away and others doing the chasing. I recognized most of the kids running as sixth graders. The ones doing the chasing? Seventh. And off just in the distance, darting up Magnolia Drive, were two skinny figures, one with a frohawk and the other with long hair pulled into a low ponytail.

Unmistakably Red. And Alejandro.

"I-I c-can't believe—" I spluttered.

One look at Isaiah told me he couldn't, either.

Go with the Flow

Chapter 5

I could not wrap my mind around it. Red and Alejandro pelting sixth graders with water balloons? My brand-new backpack was soaked, including the homework I'd already started when Ms. Tottenham gave us free time at the end of class. And Isaiah . . . he was having a hard enough time branching out without someone ruining his new book. I was so steamed, I was surprised the heat of my anger hadn't dried me off by the time I got home.

I made sure to leave my soppy sneakers and socks out on the porch before I stormed inside and locked the door behind me. The house was dark. Daddy was still at work, Mama at Liberty. And Red? *Oooh, Red, just you wait!*

And I did just that. Since tonight was going to be what I called a Double Whammy Monday at Liberty—poetry group *and* dance class—I changed into my ballet clothes, dried my hair, and sat down on the living room couch beside Maya, waiting for Red so I could give him a piece and a half of my mind.

"Can you believe him, Maya?" I cried as I scratched her behind her ears.

Maya only purred, but since Red had the habit of bursting into rooms all the time and scaring the fur off of her, I knew Maya was on my side—even if she couldn't say it.

I went to grab my phone from my still-damp backpack, ready to text Teagan. But she'd already texted me first: *How was your first day?*

U won't believe what Red did.

She wrote back seconds later.

What?

He and a bunch of 7th graders pelted 6th graders with water balloons. Alejandro did, too.

Teagan texted me back about a million angry-face emojis.

And Aaliyah is in my social studies class.

What?! But there was only an 8% chance! Don't worry, Gabby. You can handle her. Remember fifth grade?

I tried to imagine Teagan squeezing my hand like she did whenever Aaliyah called me Repeat; tried to imagine Teagan saying, "Ignore her, Gabby." But all that felt so long ago already.

How am I supposed to handle Aaliyah without you?

I stared down at the question on my phone, a lump forming in my throat. Quickly, I deleted it and typed *How was your first day?* instead.

A small part of me was hoping it had been terrible, so terrible, in fact, that Teagan would decide to abandon Main Line Tech completely and come to Kelly after all. Teagan would know how to handle Aaliyah *and* Red.

My phone vibrated. *It was awesome! My science teacher invented this super-special type of glue that NASA uses. NASA! How cool is that?*

I started to feel like I was still wearing my heavy wet clothes. I took a deep breath and texted back, *Super cool!*

IKR? I still can't believe Red and Alejandro, though!

Neither can I. See you later at poetry group.

The more I thought about it, the more mad I got. Red and Alejandro were usually the type of friends I could count on to be there for me when other people weren't. The whole poetry group was like that. Whenever I was with my poetry friends—who never laughed at my stutter and always waited for me to find my words—there was nowhere else I wanted to be.

And Red—Red definitely knew Isaiah and I were nervous about this school year. How could he do this?! I had so many words inside me that I just needed to get *out*. I thundered up the stairs to my room, taking the steps two at a time, and then found my journal exactly where I'd left it on my furry chair.

Back when she first started working with me for speech therapy, Mrs. Baxter had suggested I use a journal to write down all the words I wanted to say but couldn't because of my stutter. I did, at first, but last year after we started the poetry group, I found myself filling the notebook up with poems more and more until it became just that: my poetry journal.

I sat down on my furry chair, opened up to a fresh page, wrote RED in all caps at the top, and began to write. By the time I was done, I'd filled up almost two whole pages. I could've written two more, but I heard the front door open. Red! I jumped to my feet, raced downstairs, and ran right into Mama.

"Whoa, Gabby, where's the fire?" she said, laughing.

"Where's Red?" I demanded, caught a glimpse of Mama's raised eyebrow, and quickly changed my tone. "Is he in the car?"

Mama shook her head. "He texted me after school and asked if he could go to Alejandro's house."

Of course he did, the sneaky, water-balloon-throwing coward!

"Mr. Gomez is going to drop the two of them off at Liberty in time for poetry group. Are you ready?"

I was more than ready.

When Mama and I got to Liberty, she stopped at dance studio two to prepare for her Tiny Tots class and I kept on going to studio six. The whole group—Red, Teagan, Isaiah, Alejandro, and Bria—was already there.

Normally, before the official start of the meeting, we would be sprawled on our bellies on the floor, close enough for our elbows to touch, our poetry notebooks open in front of us as we read over our old poems or put finishing touches on anything new.

But today, only Bria, Alejandro, and Red were talking. Isaiah only had eyes for his still-soggy book of black activist poets, and Teagan was alternating between writing in Cody and glaring at Red and Alejandro.

I took a seat between her and Isaiah, who glanced up, gave me a weak smile, and went back to his book.

"All right, poets, let's get this word flowin' goin'!" Red said, clapping his hands.

"Did you give Red a piece of your mind?" Teagan whispered just as Red asked if any of us had any new poems to share.

"I'm about to," I whispered to Teagan, and thrust my hand into the air.

"Okay, cuz!" said Red. "Liking your enthusiasm."

Alejandro nodded in agreement. They were both smiling. How on earth could they act like they hadn't just soaked Isaiah and me with water balloons three hours ago?! The wave of emotions was back, and this time it broke over me with such force, I all but shouted, "I-It's a f-first dr-draft."

"First draft," Alejandro, Bria, and Red shouted back, matching what they must have still thought was enthusiasm. Isaiah and Teagan, on the other hand, were much quieter.

I took a deep breath and began to read.

"Let me tell you about a boy named Clifford
Poet, comedian, so I thought he was different
Thought he meant well, that he had my back

Til I was walking home one day and SMACK
Right in the face he hit us with water balloons
Took off running, his buddy Alejandro, too
Oh, yes indeed, that boy named Clifford
Got to seventh grade and yes, he *is* different
Not in a good way, oh no not at all
Now he might laugh if you trip and you fall
Let me tell you about Clifford and the way that
he was
Because after today, I hardly know you, *cuz*."

My heart pounded as I read the last word and looked up. Only Teagan and Isaiah applauded, slightly defiant looks on both of their faces. I chanced a look at Red. He stared back at me, openmouthed and wide-eyed. I waited for him to say something. He looked like he was waiting for me to do the same. In the end, it was Alejandro who said, "We didn't mean anything by those water balloons. It's just part of the tradition!"

Of all the things I'd expected either of them to say, that hadn't even made the list.

"Tr-Tradition?" I asked.

"Sixth-Grade Initiation," Bria put in, her bushy ponytail bobbing. "It's been going on for years at Kelly."

"You were involved, too?" Teagan asked Bria, a note of disgust in her voice.

"Yes," Bria replied defensively. "They're just harmless pranks the seventh and eighth graders play on the sixth graders to welcome them to the school."

"If that was your idea of a welcome, I'd hate to see what you guys would do if you *didn't* want us there," Isaiah muttered, shaking his head.

"But it's not like that," Alejandro cried. "It's supposed to be funny. Other sixth graders were laughing today. It happened to Bria and me last year, too, and we laughed."

Red nodded in agreement.

"Y-You weren't even here at the be-beginning of school last year!" I said.

Red and Aunt Tonya lived almost a half hour away. Up until he moved in with Mama, Daddy, and me that past February, he'd been going to sixth grade at a totally different school.

"I *heard* the sixth graders had fun," Red replied. "Sure, everyone said that they were surprised at first, but then it was funny. It's just water balloons."

"Just water balloons to you, maybe," I said. "But what if you'd had a pretty good day," I added. "A b-b-better day than you were expecting, for the most part, and were thinking sixth grade might not be so scary after all, and th-th-then *your own cousin and friends* ruined your hair and your homework and—"

"And what if . . ." Isaiah added, pausing as though gathering the strength to say what he had to say next. "What if you'd been bumped into accidentally-on-purpose by seventh and eighth graders the first day of school *and* they'd made fun of you for your haircut, and *then* you were pelted with water balloons, too? Would you still have laughed then?"

The poetry group went silent. I had no idea seventh and eighth graders had been bothering Isaiah today. Why hadn't he told me?

"I don't know who those kids are, Isaiah," Red said quietly, "but I'm sorry they were acting like that." He looked at me. "And I'm sorry about ruining your first day."

"Me, too," said Bria.

"I am, too," added Alejandro.

"Okay," Teagan cut in, "but last I checked, initiations aren't just one and done. So, are there more pranks coming up?"

The seventh graders exchanged another three-way look. Teagan, Isaiah, and I exploded at the same time.

"You can't be—!"

"It's not—!"

"Wh-Why w-would—!"

Red held up his hands as though trying to shield himself from the force of our words. "Yes," he said, "there are more pranks coming up." Teagan, Isaiah, and I opened our mouths to protest again, but Red barreled on, talking more loudly now. "But it really is all in good fun."

I fixed Red with my most convincing *You've-Got-To-Be-Kidding-Me* face.

"We promise," Alejandro added.

Isaiah and Teagan's expressions matched mine.

"It is," Red insisted.

I took a deep breath and let it out like Mama always does when she's stressed. It did seem like Red and Alejandro were sorry about the water balloons. I was still steamed, but these were the friends I'd written a haiku about only last week:

My poetry group
If I could will time to freeze
I'd stay here with you

If I was being totally honest with myself, I didn't really believe they would do anything so horrible it would make our lives miserable.

"Www-When d-does it get-get f-fun?" I asked.

"When you go with the flow," Bria said.

I turned to Isaiah. Was he willing to go with the flow? He shrugged, as if he'd read my mind.

"How about this?" Red said, his old Red spirit coming back. He wriggled his eyebrows. "We'll go easy on the two of you. I mean, you are my friend, Isaiah, and, Gabby, you're my cousin. And, it turns out, you've got an acid tongue."

Everyone laughed, even me.

"Think of it as Diet Sixth-Grade Initiation," Red went on. "All the same flavor, but with a lot less of the bad stuff. Not that there's any real bad stuff," he added quickly.

Red's eyes met mine. "Sorry," he mouthed again. He looked it. And maybe he, Bria, and Alejandro were right. Maybe Sixth-Grade Initiation was Kelly's weird way of welcoming sixth graders, and Isaiah and I just needed to go with the flow.

After poetry group ended, I raced over to studio four for our first ballet class of the year with my second-favorite instructor in the world (after Mama), Amelia Sanchez. Amelia was already at the barre, warming up with a few of the other girls. She flashed me a smile in the mirror and tapped her index finger to the tip of her nose, the secret code we'd shared ever since we'd first met four years ago, when I was six and she was nineteen. That nose tap meant thank you, hello, good-bye, and everything in between.

After the day I'd had, I couldn't get my sweats off and ballet shoes on fast enough. I needed to move. I found my place at the barre—the same spot I'd been using since I was six years old—and began to warm up.

My body was stiff at first, but by the time the class got to tendus, I was loosening up, the tension from this afternoon falling away with each port de bras. The more I danced, the lighter I began to feel, as if I were pulling off layer after heavy layer of sopping wet clothes. The water balloon incident started to feel like it wasn't hours ago, but days. And had I really been in social studies with Aaliyah just that afternoon?

It has always been that way for me. The dance studio could make the rest of the world disappear until it was just me and the music. Mama called it being "a natural dancer." She used to tell me that when I was a baby I even slept with one leg in passé.

It wasn't long before we'd finished barre exercises, petit allegro, and adagio, and Amelia instructed us to spread out so we could work on turns.

"We're practicing fouettés again tonight," she declared.

A few of the other girls groaned. A fouetté turn was one of the hardest turns in ballet. A full pirouette, then a plié on the standing leg while the working leg extends out to the side for a split second before it comes back into passé for another pirouette. It required concentration, a steady spot, and, as Amelia always told us, Grade A Posture.

You've got this, I told myself.

And I thought I did, but maybe the day's events *were* still throwing me off, because Amelia appeared at my side mid-turn and said, "You're looking a teensy wobbly, Gabby."

At the sound of those words, I missed my spot, wobbled even more, and fell over to the side. Amelia tapped her index finger to her nose and whispered, "Tighten your core. Grade A Posture."

Annoyance flared up inside me and my face grew hot. I *knew* all of that. And I knew how to do a fouetté turn, too. At least I thought I did. For a moment my spirits sank—I couldn't remember the last time Amelia had to correct me on fouettés—but then four words pushed their way into my mind: *Go with the flow.*

I found my spot again. Passé. Plié. Tighten my core. Find my spot . . .

Again.

Passé. Plié. Tighten my core. Find my spot . . .

"Now you've got it, Gabby," Amelia called out. "Perfect!"

Seemed like going with the flow made things turn out okay after all.

Twinkle Toes

Chapter 6

Even though Red, Alejandro, and Bria promised they would go easy on Isaiah and me, I couldn't help but be a little nervous the next couple of days, wondering if I'd be pelted with more water balloons, or have a KICK ME sign stuck to my back. But almost two whole days passed and nothing happened at all. Well, almost nothing. I was beginning to notice that in the hallways, even though the older kids weren't pelting the sixth graders with water balloons, they weren't exactly nice to us, either.

Sometimes the upperclassmen had the habit of stopping in huge groups to talk, clogging up the hallway. And no matter how much a sixth grader said, "Excuse me," they refused to move until they were good and ready to do so, usually just as the final bell rang, causing more than a few sixth graders to be late for class. And sometimes they'd do stuff like stop a sixth grader in the hallway and say something like, "Oooh, I love your hair" or, "Those sneakers are fire!" and just when the sixth grader would beam and say, "Thank you," the older kids would burst out laughing in the kid's face.

I saw a group of girls do this to Aaliyah on the third day of school—they stopped her to say they loved her too-perfect, too-tight bun. "It's, like, librarian chic," one of them said, a short girl with extensions dyed a deep magenta at the tips. The girl could hardly keep a straight face.

"Okay," Aaliyah said flatly.

"Aren't you going to say thank you?" the girl with the extensions asked, still smirking.

"No," Aaliyah said, in the same flat voice, "I'm not." And she walked away, leaving the girl and her two friends glaring at her retreating back.

"Who does she think she is?" the girl hissed.

"Somebody important," one of the other girls replied. "That's why she's always alone, with her no-friends-having self."

I hurried by before they decided to pay me a "compliment," too.

There hadn't been another big prank like the water balloons on the first day, though. That is, until just before last period on the fourth day of school. I was coming around the corner when I heard a boy cry out, "Hey, what's that on your locker?"

"What's that on yours?" a girl replied.

There was a sticky note stuck to the name tag on each of our lockers. I watched as one by one the kids around me peeled the small squares off and read the words on them. I did the same. My sticky note read: *Your Newbie Nickname . . .* Beneath the words was an arrow. I was about to flip the note over when a voice cried, "Oh no, not again!"

I looked up to see Ms. Tottenham hurrying down the hallway, her dreadlocks flying as she stopped to collect nicknames as she went. Some kids were giggling as they handed theirs over, while others looked like they'd been poked in both eyes.

"Boys and girls, ignore those notes. Just ignore them," Ms. Tottenham said loudly.

All I had to do was wait for Ms. Tottenham to walk up to me and take my nickname away. I never even had to know what it was. But I couldn't help myself. I flipped the note over. On the back, someone had written a word in big, thick black letters: *G-G-G-Gabby.*

My whole body jolted, like I was in the middle of a fouetté turn and missed my spot.

But then I saw that someone had crossed out that name with a pencil, and written *Twinkle Toes* in the corner. I knew that handwriting. It was Red's.

"I'll take that, Gabriela," Ms. Tottenham said, her hand already outstretched.

I smiled as I handed the note over to Ms. Tottenham. Red *was* looking out for me, just like he'd said he would. I walked into social studies, Ms. Tottenham on my heels.

Aaliyah was already in her seat. When I passed her to get to mine she cut her eyes at me, but she didn't say anything. She focused her attention on Ms. Tottenham, who now stood front and center. Today, Ms. Tottenham wore wildly patterned pants with legs so wide they looked like a skirt and, if possible, even more bracelets than before. The major difference, though, was her smile. It was still there, but nowhere as bright as it had been that first day.

"Before we begin," she said, her voice tight, "if you are still in possession of a note that was left on your locker, please give it to me."

All around me, kids pulled nicknames from their

backpacks or pockets. One kid pulled his from inside his shirt. Ms. Tottenham collected them one by one.

"Aaliyah?" she said, stopping in front of Aaliyah's desk.

"I didn't get one."

A bunch of kids turned to stare at her. Others turned to look at each other, but no one dared to say anything.

"Consider yourself lucky," Ms. Tottenham said, and made her way back over to the trash can, where she tossed in two fistfuls of sticky notes. "Now," she said, turning back to us with her usual smile, "let's talk about this." She pointed at the whiteboard, where she'd written a question: *What will you contribute to the Kelly community this year?*

She stood before us for a moment expectantly, and my insides started to jitterbug. What if she went around the room and made everyone say one thing they'd like to contribute? I hated talking aloud in front of the class, especially if I didn't have a clue what to say. But just as I was about to ask for the bathroom pass, Ms. Tottenham went over to her desk and came back with a stack of blank loose-leaf paper.

"Your name on the top and your answer below it, if you please."

"Do we have to share?" Josiah asked, and I wanted to hug him for asking.

"Not with the class," Ms. Tottenham answered, and I wanted to hug her, too.

I reached into my backpack for my pencil case just as Aaliyah reached down for hers. As she pulled her pencil pouch from her bag, a small orange square fluttered out and landed on the floor at my feet. I knew what it was at once. Aaliyah's sixth-grade nickname: Lonely—

Aaliyah slammed the toe of her shoe down on top of the note, but it was too late. I'd read the whole thing. The upperclassmen had nicknamed Aaliyah Lonely Loser. I watched, openmouthed, as she bent to snatch the note off the floor. She crumpled it up and shoved it back inside her bag.

I wanted to tell Aaliyah that I wasn't trying to be nosy. That I was sorry that the older kids had given her that name. It was true, no one really wanted to be friends with Aaliyah. They said she was too bossy. Too much of a know-it-all. And Marcus Bradley, whose mother was a part-time palm reader, said last year that the lines on Aaliyah's palms indicated that she had a lot of negative energy. Still, none of that made that mean nickname okay.

I wanted to tell Aaliyah all of this, but I couldn't find the words. Not yet, at least.

"Gabriela, let's get to work, please," Ms. Tottenham said.

I tried to focus on my paper, but I couldn't think of one single thing I'd contribute to Kelly this year, unless getting rid of the nicknames the older kids gave to sixth graders could be considered a contribution. I chanced a look at Aaliyah. She was writing feverishly, covering almost half the sheet of paper in her neat, slanted handwriting.

"Okay, now, instead of sharing with the whole class, we're going to share with one of the people around us," Ms. Tottenham called out.

Whenever it was time to pair up in fifth grade, Teagan was always right there to be my partner. Now . . . I glanced quickly to my left and then my right. The kids on either side had already partnered up with other people. My heart began to race.

I swallowed hard, wishing more than ever that it was Teagan who was turning slowly around in her seat. I looked from Aaliyah's sheet of paper, almost completely filled on one side, to my own—still blank.

"I'll go first," Aaliyah said, and began to recite what she had written. She'd contribute change, she said; she'd improve the lending policy in the school library; she'd start up a homework study buddy group for kids who needed extra help. She listed so many things, I wondered how she'd managed to come up with all of them after being in school for only four days. When she finished rattling off her list, she looked at me, raised one eyebrow, and said, "Are you going to share yours, or what?"

I folded my blank sheet of paper in half and then into fourths. "I-I d-didn't—" Aaliyah's eyes narrowed beneath her dark brows. "I th-thought you said-said y-you didn't g-get a n-n-nickname," I blurted out, as surprised to hear the words come out of my own mouth as Aaliyah was.

That wasn't what I'd meant to say!

I was supposed to say, *I'm sorry you got such a mean nickname. It wasn't right at all.*

But that's not what I'd said, and now Aaliyah glared at me and snarled, "Why don't you just mind your own business, *Repeat*?" and turned abruptly around in her seat.

"All done sharing, girls?" Ms. Tottenham asked, coming over to the two of us.

I nodded, not trusting myself to speak, seeing as how my words seemed to be malfunctioning.

"Great. Now let's see how well you listened to one another. Aaliyah, tell me one thing Gabriela wants to contribute."

"Gabriela didn't do the assignment," Aaliyah replied.

Ms. Tottenham turned to me, just as the classroom door opened and Mrs. Baxter stepped inside. "Good afternoon, Ms. Tottenham," she said. "I need to see Gabriela for speech."

"Of course," Ms. Tottenham replied, grabbing a mint-green piece of paper and a note card off her desk. She handed them to me. "To read at home, since you'll miss the end of class."

I gathered my pencil case and backpack as quickly as I could, but not quickly enough. Because I still heard Aaliyah whisper as I went by, "Have fun at speech, Repeat."

"I n-need to get-get r-rid of my stutter," I told Mrs. Baxter as soon as we were in her office and the door was closed behind us. My heart was still pounding, making my speech all bumpy.

Mrs. Baxter, who had been about to sit down at the circular table near the window, stopped and stared at me, hovering momentarily above her seat. "That's not the answer I expected when I asked you how your summer went." She sat down and rested both her elbows on the table, then gestured to the chair across from her with her chin.

"M-My s-summer was f-fine," I replied, sliding into the seat and taking in the office around me. At Thomas Jefferson Elementary, Mrs. Baxter didn't have an office, so we used to meet in whichever classroom was available.

"I'd say your summer was more than fine," Mrs. Baxter said. "Ms. Tottenham told me she saw you on the news."

I nodded, waiting for Mrs. Baxter to begin my breathing exercises or introduce an activity. If we were going to get rid of my stutter, we really needed to get to work.

"How long have you been coming to see me, Gabby?" Mrs. Baxter asked.

"S-Since second gr-grade."

"And do you remember what I told you that day and a few times since then about your stutter?"

Deep down, I knew. I nodded.

"Good. I want to hear you repeat it. Let's take a breath from our diaphragm, relax our shoulders, and speak on the breath."

I took in some air so it filled not just my lungs but my belly, too, and then on the exhale, I recited what she had told me since day one in speech therapy. As I did, the truth of the words pressed down on me, and my words grew bumpier and bumpier.

"My stutter is a part of me and it's nothing to be ashamed of, nothing to hide, and nothing to fix. I can work on improving it and learning how-how to better manage my b-b-bumpy speech, but it may never go-go away completely, and I n-n-need to learn to em-em-embrace it as a unique part-part-part of myself . . ."

Mrs. Baxter gave me an encouraging smile.

"And do you remember what I said at the end of last year about starting middle school?"

Now that she reminded me, I did. *Big life changes like starting middle school can make my stutter act up. That's totally normal.*

I nodded. "But if I could . . ."

"We can work on some techniques to help cope with this big transition, Gabby, but you know your stutter is part of you for good. So what's with you coming in here today saying you want to get rid of it?" Mrs. Baxter asked.

"B-Because p-people are m-making fun of me," I said, thinking of the crossed-out nickname, but mostly of Aaliyah calling me Repeat. A lump began to form in my throat. I swallowed hard against it.

"People like who?"

I hesitated. I knew if I told Mrs. Baxter, she'd pluck Aaliyah out of class right that very second, demand that she apologize, and make things worse. "J-Just people," I muttered.

"Well, what have we said you should do when 'just people' make fun of you?"

I swallowed again, then recited each strategy Mrs. Baxter had taught me, ticking them off on my fingers as I went.

1. Ignore the teaser.
2. Walk away.
3. Respond with humor. (Mrs. Baxter's personal favorite was to reply, "Wow! I stutter? I had no idea!")

When I was done, she leaned back in her chair and heaved a great sigh. "Good. I was beginning to think you'd forgotten everything I've taught you all these years, Gabby," she said, smiling.

I tried to manage a smile back, but I couldn't just yet.

We sat there in silence a minute or two, and then Mrs. Baxter said, "You know, Gabby, one thing that might make this transition easier is you getting involved in some school activities—make a place for yourself here. Have you thought about running for Sixth-Grade Ambassador?" She pointed to the mint-green flyer I'd put down on the table.

I shook my head.

"The student body elects one ambassador for each grade to serve as the voice of his or her class," she explained. "After the election, the ambassadors meet with the principal and vice-principal once or twice a month to talk about the issues facing their peers. The purpose of this program is to bring about change at Kelly Middle School."

It sounded a little like what I had done at Liberty this summer, which was actually pretty fun, but how would I do that—who would vote for me, with my stutter? I tried to imagine it.

"Impossible," I said.

"Gabby." Mrs. Baxter turned her chair to face me square on. "Did you ever think you would be on TV this summer talking to thousands of people?"

I shook my head again. "That was different. I couldn't see those people, didn't have to talk to them in the hallways every day."

"I'll tell you something, Gabby," Mrs. Baxter said. "See that shirt up there?"

A T-shirt with the words of a man named Saint Francis

of Assisi was thumbtacked to the bulletin board: *Start by doing what's necessary; then do what's possible; and suddenly you are doing the impossible.*

"That quote has always reminded me of you."

I gave her a sideways look. *Me?*

"Gabby, repeat after me," Mrs. Baxter said. "My name is Gabriela McBride. I stutter and it's okay."

Mrs. Baxter hadn't made me say that chant with her since we'd started meeting back in second grade. My face grew hot at the thought of doing it now. I was ten, not six. But I remembered how powerful the chant had made me feel back then, and I needed to feel a little powerful now.

"M-My n-name is Gabriela McBride," I whispered. "I st-stutter and it's okay."

"Again."

"My n-name is Gabriela McBride. I st-stutter and it's okay." My voice was a little louder that time.

"Once more."

This time my voice burst out of me and soared around the room like it had wings. "My name is Gabriela McBride. I stutter and it's okay."

Mrs. Baxter stared across the table at me. "Is it?" she asked.

"Yes. It is."

I met Isaiah outside on the front steps after school. I was about to tell him what had happened with Aaliyah when a kid passing Isaiah and me waved and said, "See you later, Fakespeare."

Isaiah waved back. " 'It were a grief so brief to part with thee. Farewell,' " he replied. The kid burst out laughing and took off at a run.

"D-Did he just call-call you—" In my surprise, my bumpy speech was getting the best of me.

" 'Tried to make me stop laughin', stop lovin', stop livin'—But I don't care! I'm still here!' " Isaiah said, grinning a little.

I stared at him, trying to see if beneath the Shakespeare and Langston Hughes quotes Isaiah was just as hurt as Aaliyah about being called something other than his name. It was possible Isaiah would have liked being called just "Shakespeare," but "Fakespeare" implied that Isaiah wasn't the real thing, and if anyone was the real thing when it came to Shakespeare, it was Isaiah.

"W-Was that your sssixth-grade n-nickname?" I asked, my skin starting to prickle with anger.

Isaiah nodded, his grin fading a bit. "It was crossed out,

but the people with the biggest mouths must have seen the original name." He shrugged. "It's whatever."

It's not whatever, I thought. It would've been one thing if the nicknames had been like the water balloons, done and forgotten. But I had a feeling that was far from the case.

If I Were in Charge

Chapter 7

That night after dinner, I sat at my desk in my room, Maya curled up in my lap, and settled down to do homework. I yanked my language arts binder and then my copy of *The Giver* from my backpack. A piece of mint-green paper came out with it.

The ambassadors flyer.

Would you like to create real change at Kelly Middle School?
Then run for the role of Sixth-Grade Ambassador!

As Sixth-Grade Ambassador, you will:

- *Be the voice of your fellow sixth-grade students*
- *Attend bimonthly ambassador meetings*

- *Work with the Seventh- and Eighth-Grade Ambassadors, as well as the principal and vice-principal, to change Kelly for the better—for all students*
- *Spearhead fund-raisers and community events*

There was an arrow at the bottom of the page indicating I should turn it over.

Requirements to run for Kelly Ambassadors:

1. *Write your name, as well as why you would like to run, on the provided note card and submit it to Ms. Tottenham in Room 127.*
2. *To focus his/her campaign, each candidate must come up with a campaign platform. All students running are encouraged to generate slogans, posters, and whatever other materials he/she feels will help popularize his/her campaign.*
3. *Candidates are responsible for designing and distributing any and all campaign materials.*
4. *Each candidate must compose an original speech. Students will present their speeches at two meetings with the other candidates before the election, with the purpose of giving and receiving feedback.*

If I Were in Charge

The final speech will be presented at the school-wide Kelly Ambassadors Election Assembly on October 5.

A speech? Mrs. Baxter hadn't said anything about a speech. But I knew what I would do if I were Sixth-Grade Ambassador: Get rid of Sixth-Grade Initiation once and for all. No more water balloons. No more nicknames. No more of anyone making sixth graders feel unwelcome at Kelly at all.

What if I did it? What if I ran for the role of Sixth-Grade Ambassador?

Forgetting all about poor Maya, I jumped to my feet. She fell gracelessly to the floor and crouched there, glaring up at me, her tail lashing.

"Sorry, Maya!" I cried, but I couldn't worry about her just then. Not until I knew the answer to the question I'd just asked myself.

And I knew just who could help me answer it. I opened up my laptop and called Teagan on video chat. She picked up, slightly bleary-eyed and yawning.

"Did I wake you up?" I asked. It was a little after eight, and I couldn't remember the last time Teagan had made it to bed before ten. She liked to stay up coding, or, as Mr. Harmon said, "Burning the midnight oil."

"No. I'm just doing some homework."

"Looks like you've got a mountain of it," I said. Part of the screen was obscured by a pile of books at least ten inches high, and Teagan was clearly in the middle of an assignment. She faced the camera, but her eyes were still on the paper in front of her.

"Teagan?"

"Sorry, Gabby," she said, tucking her pencil behind her ear. "I'm listening now. Can you repeat whatever you just said?"

"I was just going to—" but I had lost my train of thought. Teagan saying "repeat" had sent me right back to this afternoon in social studies.

By the time I was done telling her about what happened with Aaliyah, Teagan's face had turned almost as red as the pencil she had tucked behind her ear.

"Ugh, Gabby, she's awful. But—"

"I can handle her," I finished, nodding. I had Teagan *and* Mrs. Baxter in my corner. "If Aaliyah says anything to me in social studies tomorrow, I'll be ready for her. I'm gonna be all, 'Oh, do I stutter? I never noticed!' And she's gonna be like, 'Ooooh, I better leave you alone!' "

"Yes!" Teagan cried, pumping the air with her fist. She sounded fully awake now. "That's how you do it, Gabby!" She paused and looked around, her smile sagging a little. "Just like I have to do this mountain of homework." She sighed. "But where is my pencil?" Her face disappeared from view. I could hear her shuffling everything around on her desk, looking for it.

"Teagan?"

Teagan reappeared.

"Your pencil is, um, tucked behind your ear."

"Oh!"

We dissolved into giggles and ended the call a minute later.

It was only after I stopped laughing that I realized we hadn't talked about the ambassadors. I thought about texting her but didn't want to interrupt her homework again.

Could I ever be an ambassador with my stutter?

I imagined Teagan in full-on Teagan Problem-Solving Mode. She'd tell me I'd already been a leader with my stutter this summer when I'd stood up for Liberty, just like Mrs. Baxter had.

Without thinking, I went back to my desk and shoved my schoolbooks aside until I found my journal and a pen. I turned to a new page and wrote If I Were in Charge.

Gabriela Speaks Out

If I were in charge
I would fix Kelly
A school torn apart with taunts
Fears, rejection, jeers
"You don't belong"
"You're different"
"You're not welcome here"
I'd mend those rips
Those tears
Those cracks
"You do belong"
"Different is okay"
Lay those words down
Like a welcome mat
Where sixth-grade feet are free to walk
No matter their shoes
Their passions
Basketball, Shakespeare, or Langston Hughes
If I were in charge
I'd fling the door open wide
"Come in; sit down."
"You're all welcome inside."

If I Were in Charge

I marched into room 127 the next day with my note card in hand, but Ms. Tottenham wasn't standing in the doorway to greet us, nor was she standing in the center of the room in front of her desk. Instead, in that exact spot stood an older teacher with tightly coiled gray-and-white hair and a thick pair of glasses pushed down over a nose that looked stuck on her face like an afterthought.

The class was loud. Like Reading-Terminal-Market-on-a-Saturday loud. And no one was in their seat. Except Aaliyah.

"Where—" I started to ask the gray-and-white-haired teacher, but she cut me right off.

"Just take a seat. She'll be here shortly," she shouted over the noise. And then to my classmates, "Boys and girls, for the second time, do settle down. Your teacher will be here momentarily, and I want to be able to tell her that you were quiet and well behaved in her absence."

The noise lessened some, but only for thirty seconds or so, if that. Then Josiah made a fart sound, Marcus fell off his chair laughing, Zuri called them both fools, and Aaliyah got to her feet.

"Enough!" she said.

An immediate silence followed. Everyone stared at Aaliyah, even the gray-and-white-haired teacher.

"You guys are being super disrespectful," Aaliyah went on, looking directly at Josiah now. "To Ms. Tottenham and—" She turned to the teacher.

"Ms. Oliver," the teacher put in quickly, her eyes wide behind her glasses as she stared at Aaliyah in awe.

Even I couldn't help but do the same, especially after Aaliyah took her seat and the class stayed pretty much quiet. I couldn't believe Aaliyah had done that—gotten people to listen to her just with her words. With my stutter, I doubted I could ever do something like that. Not without anyone laughing before I got the words out, anyway.

My name is Gabriela McBride. I stutter and it's okay, I told myself.

Still, I felt a swell of envy that only grew when the class stayed quiet until Ms. Tottenham bustled in a few moments later.

"Now *this* looks like a class full of leaders," Ms. Tottenham declared after Ms. Oliver made a hasty exit. She went over to the whiteboard and scrawled a question across it: *What are the qualities of a leader?* Then she turned back around to face us, arms thrown out wide, inviting us to answer. All around me, kids starting throwing out responses. Soon, the board was covered with words like *patience, honesty, coolness, strength, nice sneakers* (that was Josiah), *organizational skills, good listening skills, confidence,* and *PASSION*. Ms. Tottenham wrote that last one in all caps.

When she finished writing, she read all the words aloud, nodding as she did so. Then she turned to us again and said, "You know what I think you need to be a good leader?" She held up her index finger. "Just one thing."

"Dope sneakers, right?" Josiah called out. "I knew it. Folks follow brothers with style."

"No," said Ms. Tottenham. "A voice. Anyone can lead so long as she or he has a voice." Her eyes found mine. "Gabriela, do you have a voice?"

My heart did two pirouettes. I hated being put on the spot. I nodded. Ms. Tottenham said, "Then let's hear it. Gabriela, do you have a voice?"

"Y-Y-Yes."

"Then you are a leader."

She asked four more people the same question, and when they answered yes, she told them the same thing.

"You are all leaders," Ms. Tottenham told us, "whether you're patient, organized, confident, or you have nice shoes. Because you have ideas and you have a voice."

I do have a voice, I thought, remembering our "Because"

video from this summer at Liberty. To show the city how much the center meant to the community, we had people make signs saying why they needed Liberty. "Because Liberty is where I met my best friend" was my first one, but my second one was "Because Liberty is where I found my voice." It's where I learned that even with my stutter, I could make real change. Where I learned I was a leader.

We spent the rest of class on what Ms. Tottenham called "our first big unit of study." She wrote the name of the unit—*Unexpected Leaders*—on the board and went right into teaching us about a woman named Claudette Colvin. Ms. Colvin didn't set out to be a leader; she saw injustices during the civil rights movement and stood up against them because she just had to.

I knew the feeling.

"A reminder," Ms. Tottenham said a few minutes before the end of class. "If you'd like to run for Sixth-Grade Ambassador, please return your note card to me by Monday."

The bell rang then and the ambassadors were the topic of conversation while we packed up. Josiah said he might run just so he could get the school to change the gym uniforms.

"They ride up in the, um, well, you know," he said.

"Yeah, like anyone would take you seriously enough to vote for you, Melon Head," Zuri snapped.

"Hey, how did you know about his nickn—" Marcus started, but Josiah cut him off.

"Shut up, Marcus!" he said, his face falling a little.

"I saw the sticky note on his locker before he gave it to Ms. Tottenham," Zuri said, giggling.

I couldn't believe sixth graders would call one another those mean nicknames. What did that guy Francis say? *Start by doing what's necessary.* Someone *needed* to put a stop to Sixth-Grade Initiation, and that someone was me.

I grabbed my backpack and note card and marched to Ms. Tottenham's desk.

"Ms. Tottenham?" I blurted out. She turned. "I want to run for Sixth-Grade Ambassador."

Ms. Tottenham looked as surprised by my words as I was at how they'd come out, not bumpy at all.

"I'm very happy to hear that," Ms. Tottenham replied. She was smiling as she looked through the papers on her desk. I hadn't noticed before, but Ms. Tottenham had a smile like Amelia's—seeing it made you smile, too.

She found what she was looking for at last, a peach-colored piece of paper that said *Permission Slip* across the top. “Make sure you bring that signed by your parents to our first meeting on Tuesday. That’s also when we’ll practice our speeches for the first time, so make sure you have a draft by then, okay?”

I nodded.

Ms. Tottenham smiled that contagious smile again. “I’m happy you’ve decided to run, Gabriela.”

“Me, too.”

Awesome Sauce

Chapter 8

That night was another Double Whammy Night—this time poetry group followed by hip-hop class. I had told Isaiah about my decision and platform right after school, and told Mama and Red I was running as soon as Mama picked us up that afternoon. I hadn't argued when she said the occasion deserved a pit stop for ice-cream sundaes—a double dose of chocolate sauce for me—but it meant we arrived at Liberty with just enough time for Red and me to race each other to studio six.

"I win!" said Red, slightly out of breath. Teagan, Isaiah, Bria, and Alejandro were already there. "Twinkle Toes here almost beat me."

"Yeah, right," I said. "I let you win!"

"Speaking of winning," Isaiah cut in, "Gabby has some news to share."

Red clapped his hands. "That's right, cuz!" Red said. "Tell them!"

"You didn't tell me you had big news," Teagan said. She made a pretend pouty face.

"Actually, it's huge news," Isaiah put in. "Tell them, Gabby!"

"Okay, okay!" I looked at the rest of the group and then at Teagan. "I'm running to be Kelly Ambassador for the sixth grade."

Teagan threw her arms around me and said, "OhmygoshGabbythat'ssoawesome" all in one breath. Then, calming down slightly, she said, "What are the Kelly Ambassadors?"

We all laughed and filled her in. To say Teagan was excited for me was like saying she was only okay at coding.

"We need a saying for stuff like this," she said, "for when one of us does something really big. We say 'first draft' when someone shares a new poem. What about we say . . . 'awesome sauce!' whenever someone does something amazing?"

"Let's try it," Alejandro said. "On the count of three. One. Two. Three!"

"Awesome sauce!"

It was the best sound I'd heard all week.

"I like it!" Red said, nodding. "Now, let's get down to some poetry—"

"But wait," Isaiah interrupted. "There's more. When she becomes our class ambassador, Gabby is going to work to get rid of Sixth-Grade Initiation."

"That's a great idea!" Teagan exclaimed.

Bria, Alejandro, and Red, on the other hand, were doing that talking-with-their-eyes thing Mama and Daddy always did before they said something they knew I wouldn't like.

"I thought you were over that, cuz," Red said.

Bria and Alejandro nodded in agreement.

"H-How can we be-be?" I asked, and told the three of them and Teagan all about how kids were still getting called by their mean nicknames. I didn't mention that one of these people was Isaiah. I didn't want to embarrass him all over again or let Red know that his attempts at going easy on us hadn't really worked.

"That's awful," Teagan said, glaring at the three seventh graders like it was all their fault. "Didn't you tell us at the last meeting that this initiation stuff was all in good fun?"

"It is!" Bria replied.

"Then why are people still using those nicknames?" Isaiah asked.

Alejandro shrugged. "It happens every year." He told us all about how the older kids bothered him almost as bad as they bothered Isaiah.

"But it's all good now," Alejandro said. "You get over it. They get over it. And then everything is chill."

"And anyway," Red added quickly, "Sixth-Grade Initiation is pretty much over."

"But what about next year's sixth graders?" I said. *Why should anyone have to get over being called a nasty name?*

"Look, cuz, do you want to win?" Red asked, snapping me out of my thoughts.

I nodded.

"Then you need a platform the whole school can get on board with."

Oh. Right.

It wouldn't be just the sixth graders voting for me. Every student voted for each grade's ambassador, because the ambassadors worked on issues that involved the whole school.

"Hang on," Teagan said, pulling out Cody and flipping to a new page. She looked up at Red. "I don't know if that's true."

We all waited in silence as Teagan scribbled calculations in her notebook.

"Gabby." She had entered full-on Teagan Problem-Solving Mode. "Do you think you could get most of the sixth graders on board with your platform?"

I thought back to Marcus calling Josiah his nickname yesterday. Josiah had laughed it off, but I was betting that Josiah would get rid of initiation if he had the chance. What I'd seen in the hallways throughout the week told me most sixth graders probably would. A quick look at Isaiah said he agreed.

"I don't know what the other sixth-grade candidates' platforms are yet," I said to Teagan, "but, yeah, I think I could get most of the sixth-grade votes. At least if Isaiah will help me campaign?" I turned to him.

"You bet, my lady!" Isaiah replied. I giggled.

"Okay," Teagan said. "So you're sort of already ahead. And if you're ahead with the sixth graders by a landslide, you wouldn't even need to get the same amount of votes from seventh and eighth graders as the other sixth-grade candidates do. I think you should give it a try."

"Yeah," Isaiah said. "And I bet you can count on at least three seventh-grade votes." He eyed Red, Bria, and Alejandro.

"Of course, cuz, of course," Red said.

Bria squirmed a little bit. "I still think it's risky, but we'll support you no matter what." Alejandro nodded in agreement.

Three seventh-grade votes. That was a start. I wasn't sure I followed *all* of Teagan's logic, but I knew I'd heard one thing clearly—if I could guarantee the sixth-grade votes, I'd be golden.

"I'm going to do it!" I said, sitting up straighter.

"All right!" Isaiah said.

"Yes!" Teagan added.

"That's great, cuz," Red said. "But if you change your mind about your platform, I have some unbeatable ideas. You know where to find me." He wiggled his eyebrows.

I laughed. "I'll keep that in mind."

"All right, then," Red said, clapping his hands again. "We'll get to poetry in a sec, but first, one more big 'awesome sauce' for Gabriela McBride, future Sixth-Grade Ambassador—the best Kelly Middle School has ever seen! One. Two. Three!"

"AWESOME SAUCE!!"

I bet Mama heard us all the way in studio one.

Awesome Sauce

Awesome sauce
Chocolate sauce
Welcome sauce
Go get 'em sauce
Stand up sauce
Speak out sauce
Inspire sauce
Empower sauce
Leader sauce
Speechwriter sauce
Ideas sauce
Let's do this sauce
Different sauce
It's okay sauce
You're welcome sauce
Awesome sauce

Rocking It

Chapter 9

The next few days flew by, and before I knew it, it was time for my first meeting with the other kids running for Sixth-Grade Ambassador. Today we were going to share our speeches and offer each other feedback. I grabbed my lunch from the cafeteria, waved to Isaiah, who was sitting at our table with his book and school lunch, and hurried to Ms. Tottenham's room. Teagan had helped me with my speech over the weekend, and yesterday I'd practiced with Mrs. Baxter during school and then with everyone at home, including Maya, who had thrust her tail in the air when I was done. I considered that a thumbs-up.

"You're going to rock this," Mama had said to me that morning during the car ride to school.

I was the first to arrive. Ms. Tottenham had set up a row of chairs at the front of the room, their backs to the first row of desks, and had somehow found an old wooden podium, which stood in front of the whiteboard. I took the chair closest to Ms. Tottenham's desk and pulled out my lunch.

Soon the rest of the candidates began to trickle in. This was my first real look at who I'd be up against. There was a girl named Dominique, who was obsessed with jumping double Dutch. On her heels came a boy named Darrin, who had to be the biggest sixth grader in the world. He was almost as tall as Daddy and definitely as wide, like he was born to play football. Then came the twins, Layla and Kayla, who were not identical, but made up for this fact by dressing exactly alike every day of the week.

Darrin sat down beside me and started in on what might have been his second sandwich. There were bread crusts already on his tray.

"We need bigger lunches," he said to me around a mouthful of bread, turkey, and mustard.

"Bigger?" I asked.

Darrin nodded. "I'm never going to get huge enough to be a linebacker for the Philadelphia Eagles if I keep eating these scrawny meals. Bigger lunches are part of my platform," he added, leaning in to me conspiratorially. He patted the pocket of his sweats. "Got it all right here in my speech." Then he started in on a bag of chips.

"Finish up your lunches so we can get started!" Ms. Tottenham called.

I was just popping my last carrot stick in my mouth when someone came rushing into the classroom and right up to Ms. Tottenham's desk.

"I'm sorry I'm late, Ms. Tottenham! I had a dentist appoint—"

"No worries, Aaliyah," Ms. Tottenham said.

I stopped mid-chew. *Aaliyah was running?!*

"I'm glad you're here," Ms. Tottenham continued, lowering her voice a little. "Ms. Oliver told me she believes you are a natural leader. I must say I agree."

I tried to ignore the feeling in my stomach, like I was in an elevator that had just plummeted ten floors. *A natural leader?*

Aaliyah scurried past—though not without tossing a classic Aaliyah glare in my direction—and took the seat at the very end of the row.

Darrin leaned over to Dominique and whispered, "Should have guessed Aaliyah was running. It will give her a chance to boss the vice-principal *and* the principal around."

Dominique looked just about as thrilled as I was that Aaliyah was running. "Yeah, but people listen to her." She slid down in her seat. "I'd vote for her." She said this last part so quietly, I almost didn't hear her.

We finished our lunches in silence.

A couple minutes later, Ms. Tottenham clapped her hands once and said, "Let's get started, leaders!"

As she explained to us how the speech presentations and feedback would go, I closed my eyes and imagined me giving my speech, taking belly-breaths at certain spots like Mrs. Baxter and I practiced, and then saying phrases on each exhale. With Aaliyah here, I knew I'd need to use all the techniques I'd ever learned.

"Gabriela, did you get that?"

I jumped at the sound of my name. My eyes flew open. "Get-Get wh-what?"

"The order." Ms. Tottenham pointed at the names on the board. I was fourth. Right after Aaliyah.

Uh-oh.

At once, a jitterbug started up inside of me. What if Aaliyah was so white-light amazing she made my outstanding, awesome-sauce, thumbs-up speech seem more like a dim bulb? I read my speech over again, the words as familiar to me now as those I'd heard from everyone close to me since I'd decided to run.

You're going to rock this.

You'd make a great leader.

You've got this, cuz.

I did.

Kayla and Layla were up first.

Their platform was all about Kelly's social life. They presented their speech in perfect unison and, according to what Darrin muttered under his breath, used the word "party" twelve times.

After we'd offered the twins constructive feedback, it was Darrin's turn. He delivered his speech with his paper held in one hand and the other hand cutting through the air in a fist. He said things like, "Tax dollars" and, "Lunch isn't one size fits all—why should I have to pay for two lunches?"

"Because you eat two lunches," Dominique called out.

The twins dissolved into giggles. Ms. Tottenham held her finger to her lips. When Darrin had concluded his speech with a rallying call of "Who will join me in my quest for more food?" Ms. Tottenham turned to us. "Thoughts?"

"You were very energetic," Layla said, having composed herself.

"Maybe don't move your arms around so much when you talk?" Kayla added. "It's fun to watch, but also sort of distracting."

Energy equaled good. Too much moving was bad. I made mental notes to myself, tucking them away with Mrs. Baxter's tips. *Slow down. Take your time. Say what you have to say no matter how your words sound. And remember: It's natural for a stutter to come out when you're a little nervous.*

"Aaliyah, you're up."

Aaliyah walked calmly to the podium, leaving her speech sitting on her chair. She was going to do it from memory?! I could tell from the way the other kids looked at Aaliyah—mouths open and eyes wide—that they were just as shocked as I was. The jitterbug started up inside me again, as Aaliyah began to speak.

"Good afternoon. My name is Aaliyah Reade-Johnson, and if you believe in improving Kelly Middle School—for everyone—you should vote for me for Sixth-Grade Ambassador. As ambassador, I plan to work tirelessly to turn Kelly into the school we all deserve. First, let me ask you a question. How many of you have felt too intimidated to ask your teachers for help?"

Layla thrust her hand into the air. Kayla yanked it back down.

"As Sixth-Grade Ambassador, I plan to institute a lunch-time tutoring buddy service, where students can help other students learn, eliminating the intimidation factor and upping grades in the process. I will also work on raising money for our junior varsity teams so that they can have uniforms just as nice as the varsity teams. Additionally, I will work with administration and the PTO to come up with funds so that we can have one-to-one laptops. A laptop for every student means no one is at a disadvantage just because he or she cannot afford a computer at home. Those plans are just the tip of the iceberg, however. The rest of my plan involves you and the changes *you* want, and the Kelly you wish to see. Because as Sixth-Grade Ambassador, I promise to listen to you and to be your voice so that, together, we can make Kelly the best it can be—for all of us."

There was a stunned silence. Ms. Tottenham cleared her throat and we remembered, all at once, that we were supposed to applaud. When the time came to offer Aaliyah feedback, not a single person could think of any constructive criticism to give her.

"You-You ssssounded rrrrrr-really g-good," I said, when it was my turn, my nerves—and bumpy speech—getting the best of me. How on earth was I supposed to follow *that*? I imagined Teagan sitting beside me right then. If she was there, she'd look at Aaliyah and say, "Gabby, she's good, but you can take her." And then she'd pretend to dust her shoulders off in a near-perfect imitation of Red. I smiled.

"Gabriela?" Ms. Tottenham said gently. "It's your turn."

I got to my feet and made my way to the podium.

"Make sure you make eye contact with your audience," Ms. Tottenham called.

I looked up. And right at Aaliyah, who sat back in her chair, arms crossed over her chest, waiting. It was now or never. I steadied my breathing and focused on my words, just like Mrs. Baxter always told me to. Then I began to read.

"G-G-Good afternoon. My name is Gabriela McBride, and I'm running for the role of Ssssixth-Gr-Grade Ambass-Ambassador, because I want to make K-Kelly Mmmm-Middle School the kind of place where all st-students—especially sixth graders—feel www-welcome. Ssssixth graders, how many of you got hit with water balloons on the first day of school?"

I paused and looked out at my imaginary election-day audience, picturing the whole sixth grade raising their hands, then turned my focus to today's audience. I couldn't read the expressions on their faces, but Layla and Kayla, plus Darrin and Dominique, all raised their hands. Aaliyah crossed her arms tighter. I took a breath from my diaphragm and continued.

"Ssssixth, seventh, and ei-eighth graders—h-h-how many people felt unwelcome when those nicknames were put on the lockers, either this year or the year you first started at K-K-Kelly?"

Again, I paused, this time imagining the whole sixth grade, plus some seventh and eighth graders, raising their hands. Again the twins, plus Dominique and Darrin, raised their hands. For a split second, I wondered why Aaliyah hadn't raised hers, but then I remembered that she told everyone she hadn't received a sticky note. She stared at me as if daring me to say otherwise. I put my eyes back on my speech.

"If-If-If you vote for me for Sixth-Grade Ambass-Ambassador, I will do everything in my power to get rid of Ssss-Sixth-Grade Initiation so that K-K-Kelly is a place where everyone feels welcome. If you www-want to lay d-d-down the welcome mat and invite everyone in-inside, on October fifth, vote for me, Gabriela McBride!"

That hadn't been nearly as good as when I'd said my speech for Maya, or even Mrs. Baxter or Mama and Daddy. But it hadn't been awful, either. Right?

"Let's offer Gabriela feedback," Ms. Tottenham said. "First, something positive."

"Um, well." Layla looked down at her hands.

"Gabriela had good eye contact in the beginning," Darrin offered quickly.

"You sounded positive," Kayla said.

"And upbeat," Layla added.

Dominique said, "And it's about time someone got rid of Sixth-Grade Initiation."

I thought my heart would soar right out of my chest. Maybe I actually had a tiny chance of winning against Aaliyah.

"Now, something constructive. Dominique, why don't you start?"

"Okay. Maybe practice more so you're not so nervous?"

"Aaliyah?"

"It was okay," Aaliyah said flatly, but the word had never sounded less okay than when Aaliyah said it. It seemed to hit the floor with a dull thud. My smile melted off my face.

"That's not really feedback Gabriela can use," Ms. Tottenham said.

Aaliyah shrugged, refusing to say another word.

Ms. Tottenham shook her head, her lips pursed. "Let's remember for our next meeting that we are here to help one another, and to do that, we need to be able to offer targeted and specific feedback." She pushed her chair back and stood up. "And make sure you keep practicing. The election is only two weeks away."

I made my way slowly back to my seat and flopped down into it.

"Ignore Aaliyah," Darrin whispered. "I mean, she's awesome at this, but we can't all sound like Martin Luther King. You were good." He tore open his second—or possibly third—bag of chips just as the bell rang.

People scattered, but the zipper on my backpack was stuck. Pretty soon it was just Aaliyah and me left in the classroom. She walked over to where I was sitting.

"Are you sure you have what it takes to be an ambassador, Repeat? Giving a speech in front of the whole school with that stutter . . ." She went silent, but she looked like she was trying not to laugh.

Respond with humor, Gabby, I reminded myself. I put on my cheesiest smile and shoved my hands into my pockets. "Oh, do I stutter? I never noticed!"

This time Aaliyah laughed, but I couldn't tell if it was the good kind. "Whatever," she said, shaking her head. "Just think hard about it. You wouldn't want to do anything you regret." She turned and strode out the door.

I tried not to let her words get to me and hurried off to math.

Rocking It

That night, after I'd finished my homework, Teagan came over to help me with my campaign flyers. She had Cody in hand, beanie in place, and a book bag the size of a boulder strapped to her back.

A giant smile spread across my face. "Are you spending the night?" Weekday sleepovers with Teagan were rare but not unheard of. Mr. Harmon sometimes went to visit his older sister in a nursing home a few hours away.

Teagan went pink. "Well, no. I brought over some homework, just in case you wanted to, you know, like—"

"Do more homework?" I stared at her.

She nodded, going pinker still. Then said quickly, "Just have another mountain to climb, is all."

It was still pretty warm out and the sun hadn't gone down yet, so we grabbed some of Mama's delicious homemade chocolate chip cookies and my laptop and settled down on the back porch. Teagan slid her backpack off. It hit the floor beside her with a pretty big thud.

"How's school going?" I asked, eyeing her book bag warily.

"It's awesome!" Teagan cried, taking a gulp of her lemonade. "I mean, it's a ton of work—a *ton*—but I love it. My coding teacher is talking about teaching us Pascal, which is, like, one of the hardest coding languages to learn."

Teagan went on, talking about code. Physics. Parabolas. She may as well have been speaking in an alien language for all I understood, but I nodded and couldn't help but smile whenever Teagan did. She had the kind of happiness that reached out and grabbed you, no matter how you were feeling.

"So," Teagan said at last. "Let's get started on these flyers."

"Okay," I said, opening up a new document on my laptop. "We have to make them over-the-top awesome sauce, because guess what?"

"Aaliyah's running?"

My mouth dropped open. "What? How did you know that?!" Leave it to Teagan not to even go to my school and still know what was going on there.

"A little birdie told me. Then he quoted Shakespeare."

I laughed. "Well, it's true. Aaliyah's running and her speech is amazing." I told her all about the practice speech session.

"Well, she might be good at giving speeches, but you can take her, Gabby. You've got good ideas—it doesn't matter if they come out bumpy. Besides, you've got a team of the best poets in Philly to help you with slogans." Teagan grinned, and wriggled her eyebrows in a perfect imitation of Red.

Teagan and Darrin were right. Aaliyah was awesome at giving speeches, but I wasn't so bad myself, even with my bumpy speech. I just needed more practice. And then I'd be awesome, too.

If Speaking Were like Dancing

Chapter 10

Brrrrriiiiinnngg. Brrrrrriiiinnngg.

I slammed off my alarm and tried to shake the dream I'd just had. Something about a superhero named Natural Leader saving the day. The figure had a perfect bun I knew all too well. I guess Ms. Tottenham's words to Aaliyah had gotten to me a little more than I'd realized.

There are natural leaders, I told myself. *But there are unexpected ones, too.* I repeated that over and over to myself as I brushed my teeth and got dressed, and again while I ate breakfast. I repeated it in the car on the way to school, and as I waited for Isaiah on the front steps.

I had my campaign flyers in hand—we were going to spend some time before homeroom hanging them up around the school, and then do what Isaiah called "on-the-ground campaigning" in the sixth-grade hallway. (I figured I'd tackle one grade at a time. First, double-guarantee I had all the sixth-graders' support, then worry about the seventh and eighth graders.) The plan was to hand out flyers and be available to answer questions about my platform. Just the thought of it made my stomach lurch. This wasn't like my speech that I'd practiced until Maya was tired of it. I was going to have to talk to people on the fly.

I swallowed hard just as Mr. Jordan's car pulled up to the curb. Isaiah bounded up the steps toward me with a hearty, "Good morrow, my lady. Ready to spread the good word?"

"You betcha," I said, hoping that saying I was ready would make me ready.

I handed Isaiah half the stack of flyers. We made our way around the school, hanging flyers on just about every bulletin board we could find. As we approached the sixth-grade hallway, I felt myself get tense. Each flyer hung was one flyer closer to having to talk directly to my classmates.

I checked my watch—only a few minutes left before class. If we were going to do this direct campaigning, now was the time. Or, maybe if I found a couple more places to hang flyers, the bell would ring and I wouldn't have to—

"Want to end Sixth-Grade Initiation?" Isaiah said loudly to two girls passing us, holding out a flyer.

So much for being saved by the bell.

The two girls stopped mid-conversation and mid-step and stared at Isaiah, as taken off guard as I was. I had no idea if the two girls were even in sixth grade—and I doubt Isaiah did, either—but that didn't seem to bother him at all. He held out one of my campaign flyers, the one with the slogan that shouted as loudly as Isaiah just had, *Hey, want to get rid of initiation and feel welcome inside? Then on October 5, vote for Gabby McBride.*

The girls exchanged a look, and for one stomach-sinking moment, I thought neither of them would take the flyer. Then one of the girls held her hand out for it, and with a quick "thanks" they continued down the hall.

Isaiah turned to me, beaming. "Active campaigning. Far better than hanging flyers and hoping kids read them! Come on, Gabby. I know you can do it."

I can, I said to myself. And hadn't I done something similar this past summer when I'd convinced complete strangers to stop in front of Liberty and sign our petition to save the center? If I could do it for Liberty, I could do it now, to end Sixth-Grade Initiation.

Before I could chicken out, I turned and held out a flyer to the next person I saw. It was Victoria.

"What's that?" she said, frowning down at the paper.

"It's, um, I'm-I'm r-running for Sssixth-Grade Ambass-Ambassador, and—" I paused, trying to pin my words down. Victoria looked from the flyer to me, still frowning. *She's going to walk away,* I thought. *She doesn't have time for my bumpy speech.* But Victoria just looked at me, raised her eyebrows. And waited.

"And if you v-vote for me, I-I'll get rid of Sssixth-Gr-Grade Init-Initiation."

Victoria nodded. "Good. It needs to go," she said, and then, with a quick glance around, took the flyer and continued down the hall.

"She's one of the most popular girls in our grade," I whispered to Isaiah once she was a few feet away. "Maybe she'll get all her friends on board, too."

"That's awesome sauce!" Isaiah cried so loudly, he startled Victoria. She cast a glance back over her shoulder that, roughly translated, meant, *Whoa, dude. Calm it down.*

I giggled. This wasn't so hard. I made a mental note to do the same thing tomorrow in the seventh- and eighth-grade hallways. Maybe Red, Bria, and Alejandro would even help. Then, buoyed by Isaiah's enthusiasm and the most popular girl in our grade agreeing with my platform, I handed out a few more flyers, my speech a lot less bumpy than before. In a moment of what Teagan would have called "sheer, logic-less bravery," I even handed a flyer to Aaliyah when she passed us in the hall. She glanced at it but then handed it back to me.

"No thanks," she said. "Save it for someone who might actually vote for you."

Now my stomach really did sink. Right down to my shoes.

"Come on, Gabby," Isaiah said, stepping up next to me. "Let's keep mov—"

"Hey!" A boy's voice cut across Isaiah's. It was the same older boy who'd bothered him outside on the first day of school. He was talking to me but looking right at Isaiah. "Do you know that your friend Fakespeare here tried to call *Shakespeare* a rapper?"

Anger rose in me. Fakespeare *again*? Couldn't they move on? "H-H-His n-name is I-I-Isia-a-ah—"

The boy's laughter rang out, this time at me and my bumpy speech.

"It's G-G-G-Gabby!" came a voice from another older kid across the hallway.

I sucked in my breath. I didn't know anyone had seen my original sixth-grade nickname. Or maybe they hadn't. G-G-G-Gabby wasn't exactly creative.

Well, I'd show them—for Isaiah and me. I closed my eyes against the sound of laughter, the boy's loudest of all, and took a deep breath to calm myself down, just like Mrs. Baxter would have told me to. Just like a natural leader would. But before I could get a word out, there was another voice. Loud. Clear. Not bumpy at all.

"Actually, rap is a form of poetry," Aaliyah said, stepping right up to the boy. Her hands were on her hips. "And seeing as how William Shakespeare is one of the oldest and best poets in his-tor-y, who spun some of the best rhymes of all times, I would say it's not too far off to call him a grandmaster rapper." By this point, the boy's mouth had fallen completely open. So had Isaiah's. "All this you would know, of course, if you turned off the radio once in a while and picked up a book."

All around us, lockers stopped slamming, until the hallway was as silent as our social studies class had been the day Aaliyah stood up and shouted them down.

My dream came rushing back to me. If Natural Leader Aaliyah had a superpower, I'd just witnessed it again.

And then she turned to me and fixed me with a glare

that sent an icy chill down my spine. "And you—how are you going to be the voice for the whole sixth grade when you can't even be a voice for your friend?"

Her words hit me like that time I slipped in hip-hop and had all the wind knocked out of me.

We stared at each other for a moment, and then with one last glare, she turned on her heel and walked away. As if a spell was broken, the rest of the students went back to their own business, too, but not before I saw some of them look at me the way Aaliyah had after the practice speech session. Like even the thought of me, G-G-G-Gabby, being ambassador was ridiculous.

My face burned and tears pushed at the back of my eyes. Why did Aaliyah have to say that here in the sixth-grade hallway? Why did she have to say it at all? Now I was certain not to get enough votes from kids in my own grade, which basically meant . . . I didn't even want to think about it.

I shoved the rest of the flyers into my backpack and wiped my eyes with my sleeve.

"Come on," Isaiah said, gesturing in the direction of our first classes.

I couldn't bring myself to look at him as we walked, silence the size of three dance studios settling down between us.

"Don't listen to her, Gabby," Isaiah said at last. "You would make a great voice for the sixth grade."

But Aaliyah would make a better one.

If Speaking Were like Dancing

I'd stop the world with my words
Shout with a grand jeté
Whisper with a fouetté turn
I'd pirouette, then switch leap
Kick-ball-change, mesmerize you with my speech
If speaking were like dancing
I'd never hesitate, never stutter
So flawless that you'd wonder
Where'd she learn to speak like that?
So smooth, so strong, so confident
If speaking were like dancing
People might hear my words and listen
If only speaking were like dancing
But I know that it isn't

A Change of Plan

Chapter 11

That night in tap class, I pounded the floor so hard, my feet were sore by the time I got home. But that pain couldn't compare to the ache I'd felt throbbing inside me since that morning. Not being able to get my words out for Isaiah was bad enough, but I hadn't even tried to stand up for myself after Aaliyah spat those words at me. How did I expect to inspire a whole school to stop bullying each other if I couldn't even stand up to the person who was bullying me?

I threw my dance bag in the corner and flopped down in my furry chair so hard it almost tipped over. Maya scurried out from underneath and ran off, but not before giving me a glare worthy of Aaliyah.

Oooooo, that glare. It made my skin prickle just thinking about it. I *knew* that even with my stutter, I could be just as good an ambassador as Aaliyah. But now she'd gone and ruined any chance I had at winning on my Sixth-Grade Initiation platform.

And to think I'd felt sorry for her when the older kids nicknamed her Lonely Loser and made fun of her hair.

Suddenly, I was so angry I couldn't even sit anymore. I sprang up, and this time the chair did tip over. I kicked it for good measure, only to remember how sore my feet were. The sound that came out of my mouth rivaled Maya's angriest yowl.

I had to find a way to beat Aaliyah. The question was, how?

"Hey, cuz." Red popped his head in my door. "Everything okay in here? I heard a noise like a raccoon fighting a—"

"It's fine," I said, picking up the chair and setting it down harder than I meant to. "I m-m-mean, it's not." As I sat back down and Red took a seat against the ladder of my loft bed, I told him all about this morning. "S-So now all those sixth-sixth graders are *sure* not to vote for me, and I just hate, hate, HATE it that Miss-Perfect-Hair, Meanest-Glare Aaliyah Reade-Johnson is going to win!"

Red laughed, which wasn't exactly the reaction I was expecting. "Look who's spinning verses in her fury again." He pointed at me.

I smiled. "Seriously, though, Red. I need to beat her. I don't know how it's possible on my platform without those sixth-grade votes, but maybe I can find a way to get more seventh- and eighth-grade votes, or maybe—"

Red was slowly shaking his head, a smug look on his face.

"What?"

"I knew it. I knew you'd come crawling back to ol' Red eventually."

What in heaven's name was he talking about?

He wiggled his eyebrows, and I suddenly remembered what he'd said at poetry group the other night. *If you change your mind about your platform,* he'd told me, *I have some unbeatable ideas. You know where to find me.*

"Can you really help me?" I asked. "Can you guarantee I will beat Aaliyah?"

Red sat up taller and looked me right in the eyes. "If you're trying to take down your enemy?" He kissed the fingertips on his right hand and then his left. "My platform is unbeatable."

"Tell me," I said, jumping down to sit on the floor beside him. "Now. P-Please."

As Red told me more about his idea, I had visions of

every single sixth, seventh, and eighth grader voting for me. This *was* an unbeatable platform.

"You're gonna need new flyers, though," said Red after we'd talked it through. "I can go get my laptop—"

"New flyers tomorrow night," I said, already at my desk and opening up my own computer. "I've got a new speech to write!"

In It to Win It

In this to win this
From start to finish
Margins? The slimmest
I'm talking landslides
The winning side
When I emerge victorious
It will be so obvious
I was in it to win it
From start to finish
And you know what?
I did it

The next day, in between classes, I took down a bunch of the flyers Isaiah and I hung the day before. I had to make room for the flyers with my new platform. My winning platform that guaranteed I'd get enough votes to beat Aaliyah. I did a pirouette right there in the almost empty hallway, not caring at all if anyone saw.

"Um, is there something you want to tell me?" Isaiah asked me later at lunch. "We hung a lot of flyers yesterday and now they're gone. What gives?"

"Well, I had to take them down because I made some small changes to my platform."

"Changes to your platform?" Isaiah repeated slowly. "What kind of changes?"

"Necessary ones. And I made changes to my speech, too." I dug in my bag for my new speech. "Maybe you can help me with it? You can give me some feedback."

Isaiah looked like I'd just asked him if he wanted to eat school lunch every day for the rest of his life. "What was wrong with your old platform?"

"It wasn't going to work," I said, putting my speech back down. "Not after what happened yesterday."

"Okay . . ." Isaiah said, still looking skeptical. "I guess let's hear your new speech."

"All right." I took a deep breath. "Here goes. Want to be able to use your phone during recess to b-blog, 'gram, and ch-check your newsfeed? My name is Gabriela McBride, and I'm look-looking out for your tech needs! You might be asking me, what does a vote for Gabby mean? Well, I'll tell you! It m-m-means cell phones at recess *and* access to online videos on the school computers! That's right. A vote for Gabby McBride means all tech, all the time!" I stopped and looked up at Isaiah. "A pretty good start, right?"

Isaiah looked like he'd just found a mystery hair in our meat loaf. "What even *was* that? You said small changes; those were huge! What happened to the other speech?"

"I t-told you. I m-made some ch-changes."

"Yeah, but that wasn't just a few changes. That was a whole new speech and a whole new platform. You're just going to forget all about Sixth-Grade Initiation? Real nice, Gabby. If there was a Shakespearean word for 'sellout' I'd use it now."

Some tap dancers started pounding in my chest. "B-B-But after what happened yesterday, I wasn't going to get enough votes with that platform. Or at least not enough votes to beat Aaliyah. And after what she ssssaid . . . I m-m-mean . . . I d-don't see why anyone would vote for me on that platform to stop all the bullying when I c-c-couldn't even stand up for you, or to Aaliyah."

Isaiah put his fork down. "Gabby. You know what Aaliyah said isn't true. You just needed a minute to find your words."

I pushed some soggy green beans around on my tray. "It's a little true."

Isaiah sighed. "What would make you feel more like a winner, Gabby? Making Kelly better for kids like us or beating Aaliyah?"

"B-Beating—" I stopped. My face grew hot. "B-Both, I g-guess. But—I figured I'd run on a d-d-different platform and show everyone that Aaliyah was wwwr-wrong about me and then maybe when I'm Ambass-Ambassador I can—"

He held up his hand as if to say, "Stop talking."

I opened my mouth and then shut it again. Here I was, trying to win against the girl who had cut me down the way that boy had cut Isaiah down—the girl who had made fun of *me* while I was trying to stand up for *him*. Isaiah should know more than anyone how much Aaliyah's words had hurt me. For the first time in a few days, I wished Teagan was here with me.

"You know," I blurted out, "if Teagan was here right now, she'd be all about helping me with my new platform."

The look on Isaiah's face told me he hadn't expected me to say that as much as I hadn't expected it to come out of my mouth. But I was on a roll.

"If you're not going to help me, I-I . . . I don't have to sit here!" I grabbed my lunch tray and other stuff and stood up. "I'll see you in math."

Sparks

Chapter 12

If Isaiah wouldn't help me with my new speech, I knew exactly who would. I took a deep breath to calm down the tappers and then knocked on Mrs. Baxter's door.

"Come in," she called.

It was kind of hard to hold on to my lunch tray and open the door to Mrs. Baxter's office, but I managed. Mrs. Baxter sat at her round table, Ms. Tottenham across from her.

"Oh," I said. "I d-didn't kn-know—"

"The more the merrier, Gabby," Mrs. Baxter said, and got up to pull out a chair for me. "What brings you here today?"

"I was wondering if you could help me with my speech for Sixth-Grade Ambassador," I said, sitting down. And then, with a quick glance at Ms. Tottenham, added, "If that's not against the rules."

"It's not," Ms. Tottenham assured me. "But what exactly is wrong with your speech, Gabriela? I thought it sounded great the other day at our meeting."

"Well, I have a different speech now. I changed my platform a little." I pulled my speech out of my backpack, and immediately Isaiah's words came back to me, as though they were written on the paper in front of me. *If there was a Shakespearean word for "sellout" I'd use it now.*

Well, if there was a Shakespearean word for being unhelpful, I'd call Isaiah *that.*

"Okay," Mrs. Baxter said. "Let's hear what you've got."

I cleared my throat and searched for a spot to look at over my teachers' heads—a trick Mrs. Baxter had taught me if I got nervous when speaking in front of a crowd. The T-shirt she pointed out that first day caught my eye. *Start by doing what's necessary; then do what's possible; and suddenly you are doing the impossible.*

Just yesterday, beating Aaliyah had seemed impossible, but that was before I had this unbeatable platform.

"Whenever you're ready, Gabby," Mrs. Baxter gently said.

Here goes, I said to myself, and began my speech. I made it all the way through, though it was a little bumpier this time because those tappers were still slamming away.

But there was something else, too. Whenever I'd read my old speech—for the first time or the hundredth—I'd felt a spark, a glow, like someone had lit a thousand tiny candles inside me. When I read my new speech, though, there weren't any sparks. Not even one. Maybe there would've been, though, if Isaiah hadn't been so negative about it.

I finished and looked at Mrs. Baxter.

"S-So?" I asked my teachers. "Wwww-What do you think? How can I improve it? I rrrr-really want to win, so I'm o-open to any and all-all feedback—"

I paused, because Mrs. Baxter and Ms. Tottenham exchanged a look like the one I already knew so well.

"We can help you with the delivery of your speech, Gabby," Mrs. Baxter said. "That's not a problem. But I *do* see a different problem here."

"Wh-What?" I asked nervously.

"Do you remember what you wrote on your index card as the reason you wanted to run for ambassador?" Ms. Tottenham looked me straight in the eye.

"B-Because I wanted to get rid of Sixth-Grade Initiation and make the school more welcoming," I mumbled. But before Ms. Tottenham and Mrs. Baxter could go full Isaiah on me, I went on, my voice a little louder. "But that platform won't get me enough votes to win. N-N-Not after . . ." I decided it probably wasn't the best idea to tell them about the incident in the hallway.

"I n-n-need a platform that appeals to ssssixth graders *and* seventh and eighth graders!"

"And that's good thinking," Mrs. Baxter said.

So what was the problem?

"Gabby," Mrs. Baxter continued. "Tell me what you did for Liberty this summer."

A wave of heat rose within me. I'd already told Mrs. Baxter about Liberty. Why was she asking to hear about it again instead of helping me with my speech? In as few words as possible, I repeated the Liberty story for Mrs. Baxter and Ms. Tottenham.

"And why were you so willing to do all that for Liberty?" Mrs. Baxter asked.

What on earth did Liberty have to do with running for ambassador?

"Think, Gabriela," Ms. Tottenham said gently.

It didn't take me long to find the answer. "Because I-I l-love Liberty . . . and it-its community."

"So much that you'd do anything for it, right?"

"Yes."

"And people could tell that," Ms. Tottenham said. "I donated to Liberty after seeing you on the news. I found it hard not to."

My heart skipped a beat. *My words had done that?*

"I guess now you see the problem, Gabby," said Mrs. Baxter. "You think you can't win on your own platform, but you're not passionate about this one."

I opened my mouth to protest. I needed to beat Aaliyah—I was passionate about that—but Mrs. Baxter held up her hand just as Isaiah had earlier. "If you really think there should be access to tech all the time, run with it. But if you don't believe in it, no one else is going to, either."

"But maybe if you can help me say the words with more . . . more sss-sparks—"

"Speech therapy can't add passion, Gabby." Mrs. Baxter made a steeple with her hands and pressed them to her nose. "Only you can do that."

Ms. Tottenham sighed. "I know you want to win, Gabby, and if you don't think you can win on your old platform, fine. But I'm not so sure you'd win on this one, either. Why don't you give that some thought, and then we'll be happy to help you with your speech."

"Earth to Gabby," Daddy said that night at dinner.

I blinked hard and then glanced around the table. Mama, Red, and Daddy had already filled their plates. I slowly took a scoop of broccoli from one of the many serving bowls parked in front of me.

"What're you thinking so hard about?"

"My platform," I said, and left it at that.

"Your new, awesome-sauce platform, cuz! Did you tell them about it?" He tipped his chin toward Mama and Daddy.

I shook my head.

He launched into a spirited summary of my tech campaign. When I was elected, I was going to make all his middle-school dreams come true, he said. He'd be able to watch videos of spoken word groups during his free period, and video-chat with Aunt Tonya during recess, which was great, because the time difference made it hard to talk in the evenings. He was talking so fast, little bits of broccoli were flying out of his mouth. And sparks were flying off of his words.

He was making good points, too. Points I hadn't had in

my speech before. Maybe if I added those in I could find the passion my teachers were talking about!

"May I be excused?"

"Already?" Mama put her fork down. "You feeling okay? You hardly ate anything."

"Totally fine," I said. I jumped up, quickly scraped my plate, and set it down in the sink. "Just excited to work on my speech!"

Daddy said something but I hardly heard him; I was already halfway up the stairs.

Ten minutes later, I had worked in all of Red's great points. I read my new-and-improved tech speech to Maya, who had skipped the furry chair for once and parked herself on my desk.

"I don't know about you, Maya," I said when I was finished, "but I'm pretty sure I felt a spark this time. Well, maybe."

Maya yawned.

"Okay, maybe still zero sparks," I admitted to her with a sigh, rubbing her behind the ears. "Maybe if I add more exclamation points?" I reached for my pencil, but Maya had rolled over on top of it, hoping I'd scratch her belly. I gently nudged her.

Acting like I'd full-on shoved her, she jumped off my desk as if to say, "What ever happened to excuse me?" As she did so, a piece of paper fluttered to the ground.

My Sixth-Grade Initiation speech. I picked the paper up.

"It can't hurt just to read it one more time," I said to Maya, who was too busy settling down on her favorite chair to pay me any mind.

"Good afternoon. My name is Gabriela McBride, and I'm running for the role of Sixth-Grade Ambassador, because I want to make Kelly Middle School the kind of place where all students feel welcome."

Immediately I felt the flicker of a spark. Relief washed over me, and then faded just as fast.

Red wanted those tech things, and I wanted those things for Red, but not as much as I wanted Kelly to be a welcoming place for everyone. I didn't want to say the words, but I knew in the end I would have to: The tech platform was a lost cause.

"So now what, Maya?" I said. "What am I supposed to do?"

Maybe writing things out would help. I found my poetry journal on my desk and pulled out a pen.

I run on my old platform—Passion, good speech, but sixth graders won't vote for me—not after what Aaliyah said in the hallway.

I run on my new platform—No sparks . . . so not enough votes.

No winning = no beating Aaliyah, and no showing the school I'm the leader Aaliyah says I'm not.

Teagan always said there was no such thing as an impossible problem, but this one seemed pretty close to me. I checked the clock—probably a little too late to call Teagan now. I'd talk to her at poetry tomorrow—she'd know what to do.

A Solution to an Impossible Problem

Chapter 13

"Okay, that's all for today, poets," Red said, clapping his hands at the end of poetry on Friday. "We'll finish a little early tonight."

I had seven minutes until hip-hop. Could an impossible problem be solved in seven minutes? Maybe, with Teagan. But first I wanted to apologize to Isaiah. That afternoon at lunch, Isaiah had already had his nose in his newest poetry book by the time I sat down at our table. I tried to tell him how he'd been right—I'd been a total sellout, but he hadn't looked up all period, and I couldn't blame him.

I put my journal away and stood up, only to find that Isaiah was already gone. I guessed I'd try to video-chat with him later.

Teagan was still here, though, dragging her ten-ton backpack toward me. She'd arrived at poetry late, saying something about losing track of time while doing homework. Between my election stuff and her schoolwork, we'd hardly talked all week. Just seeing her here in front of me made me feel lighter, like I could do a switch leap and nail the landing without making any noise at all.

Teagan, on the other hand, looked exactly like she'd been carrying around a boulder-sized backpack all week. Her footsteps seemed heavy. Her *hair* seemed heavy, if that was possible.

"Teagan?" I asked as she let go of her backpack. "Are-Are you okay?"

She nodded. Then shook her head. Then nodded again.

I blinked. Teagan's lip was quivering. Without thinking, I reached out and put a hand on her arm.

"I . . ." she started. "I think it was a mistake to go to Main Line."

What? Of all the things I expected her to say, that was *not* one of them.

"Okay," I said. "Sit. Tell me what's going on."

We found a spot against the wall under the ballet barre where I'd gotten a massive charley horse in ballet class last spring. Teagan seemed like she was in as much pain now as I was that day. I scooted closer to her until our knees were touching and waited for her to share more, knowing how important it was to give someone time to find their words.

After a few moments, Teagan tilted her head back and leaned it against the well. "I just . . . This Pascal coding is killing me. It's so much more advanced than anything I've done." She took a deep breath. "When I got into Main Line, I knew it would be hard, but I didn't know it would be this hard. I feel . . . I feel like I'm having to prove myself every single second. My grandpa is always saying I'm a natural whiz kid—"

"You are. Like how Mama says I'm a natural dancer." I squeezed her hand. *And how Aaliyah is a natural leader,* I added to myself.

"But . . ." she continued, pulling her knees up and wrapping her arms around them. "These students are so smart, especially the ones in my coding class. I'm starting to think . . ." The next words seemed like they were some of the hardest words Teagan had ever had to say. "To think that I'm not meant to be a coder after all."

I let out a breath. I'd never seen Teagan this upset about school—or anything, really. I scooted around to face her square on. "Teagan," I said, "you have a notebook exclusively for writing code. That you named Cody. And you had that before you went to Main Line."

"I know." She sniffled. "But everyone there is so much smarter than me. I'm never going to be even close to the top of my class."

I thought back to that day in August when Teagan had told me about Main Line. How excited she'd been. How I hadn't for even one second thought she shouldn't go, even if it meant she wouldn't be with me at Kelly. Coding was Teagan's thing—it's what made her Teagan. She'd still be a coder even if she'd never heard of Main Line and had come to Kelly. She'd still be a coder even if every single person in the class was smarter than her. There was only one way Teagan wouldn't be a coder. I put my hands on her knees.

"Teagan, the only way you couldn't be a coder was if you didn't code. If you didn't do this thing you're so passionate about. Who cares if you're at the top of your class? *You* know you're a coder. *I* know you're a coder. You don't have to prove that to anybody—"

I stopped. Because I'd just realized the solution to my impossible problem.

"Gabby? Were you finished?"

I snapped my attention back to Teagan. "Oh, yeah. Did that help?"

She nodded. "It did. Thanks, G." She squeezed my hand and then pulled me into a hug. When we were done, I scooted back around next to her.

Shoot! The clock over the studio door said I was going to be late for hip-hop!

I grabbed my bag. "I have to go—are you gonna be okay?"

"I think so," Teagan said. "It will at least help me get through the insane amount of homework I have this weekend. Let's talk after poetry group on Monday. I want to hear more about your campaign!"

"You got it," I said. I hugged Teagan and ran to studio three, quickly changed my shoes, and jumped in to join the other dancers in our warm-up.

Forty-five minutes later, we had done our isolations and learned tonight's hip-hop combination. Mama counted us in.

"Five, six, seven, eight!"

I put all my energy into the moves, just like I had at the park performance for Liberty this summer.

Stomp together, hit, and slide.

Tonight, I was speaking with my body, but inside, my words pounded with each beat.

Teagan was a coder. She didn't have to prove that to anybody.

Swing my arms to the right and PUNCH!

Just like I didn't have to prove I was a leader. Not to Aaliyah, not to those kids in the hallway, and definitely not to myself.

Pump one, two! Jump three, four!

Maybe I wouldn't win.

Big step right, stop, and hold.

But that wasn't the point.

This summer when I'd choreographed that dance for the park, I didn't know if it was going to raise enough money for Liberty's building repairs.

Head to the left and pop, pop.

In fact, I knew it probably wouldn't.

Slide on six, hold seven, eight.

But I knew I had to try.

Because leaders don't wait for the impossible to be possible.

Front and back and front and back.

They start by doing what's necessary.

I was as passionate about making Kelly better for kids like Isaiah and me as I had been about saving Liberty.

Maybe I'd lose the election.

Maybe Sixth-Grade Initiation would continue for another year.

Maybe Aaliyah would call me Repeat for the rest of my middle-school career.

"Get ready for the ending!" Mama said.

But I had to give it a shot.

My name is Gabriela McBride, I thought as I spun and then jumped my legs into the widest stance I could, freezing in the final pose.

I have a voice, and I'm going to make sure all of Kelly hears it.

At home, I went straight to my desk and pulled out my journal:

Old goal: Win the election so I can get rid of Sixth-Grade Initiation.

New goal: Use my platform and speech to speak out about Sixth-Grade Initiation. Inspire people to treat each other with respect, whether I win or not!

Immediately that same spark I felt last night when I read my old speech ignited within me. If even just one seventh or eighth grader heard what I had to say and changed the way they treated sixth graders, I'd consider that a win.

Maybe some sixth graders would start treating each other better, too.

And Aaliyah? Mrs. Baxter had told me to ignore the bullies, so that was exactly what I planned to do from now on. Ignore Aaliyah and her campaign. I needed to focus on getting the word out about mine.

If I was going back to do that, though, I needed new flyers. With teeth brushed and my pj's on, I opened up my laptop and got to work, Maya "helping" me by using the keyboard as her personal pillow. I was just about to hit PRINT when a new e-mail alert popped up. It was from Isaiah.

> Gabby,
>
> I came across this poem at lunch today. It's the only poem Ernest P. Boyd ever published. I don't know what you decided about your platform, but I thought the poem might help you in your campaign.
>
> Isaiah

Of course Isaiah would have a poem to help me, even though I hadn't had a chance to apologize. A frown spread across my face at how rude I'd been to him yesterday. I scrolled down and read on.

"Bridges" by Ernest P. Boyd

Brother, I have seen
So many bridges burned
Instead of bridges built
Where there should be binds as strong as oak
There's desolation, fire, flame, and smoke
But, brother, now you listen to me
To every word I've said
For glorious this world would be
If men stopped burning bridges
And held out their hands instead

Isaiah's question from yesterday came back to me. *What would make you feel more like a winner, Gabby? Making Kelly better for kids like us or beating Aaliyah?*

So many bridges burned . . . I understood now why Isaiah was so upset yesterday. I claimed I wanted to get rid of all the teasing and tearing down at Kelly, but in switching platforms just to beat Aaliyah, I had taken part in the exact thing I was trying to stop. A wave of shame washed over me, but just as quickly, I felt the warmth of gratitude fill its place.

I opened up a new e-mail and hit REPLY.

Dear Isaiah,

Thank you for the poem—I liked it a lot. Thanks, too, for trying to help me yesterday. I was so hurt by what happened with Aaliyah that I forgot why I was running in the first place. You're a true friend for calling me out on that. And I'm sorry for what I said about wishing Teagan were there. Like I said, you're a true friend, and I'm so glad you're here at Kelly with me.

I continued by telling him how I was going back to my old platform—how even if I didn't win, maybe I'd inspire at least some students to treat each other with more kindness. I also asked if he wanted to help me hand out flyers in the seventh- and eighth-grade hallways on Monday.

Later, as Maya and I snuggled into bed, my phone buzzed. A text from Isaiah.

I would be honored, my lady, to help you spread the word.

And then another one: *And I agree wholeheartedly. As the Bard would say, "I am wealthy in my friends."*

Doing the Impossible

Doing what's impossible
Means jumping
Even when you think you'll fall
It means running headlong
Straight through the wall
Doing the impossible
Means looking your fears straight in the face
Saying loud and clear, "You will not win today."
It means dropping the "i" and the "m"
It means trying, failing
And getting back up again

Building Bridges

Chapter 14

"Ladies and gentlemen," Ms. Tottenham said on Monday after the bell rang. "This week we will review what we've learned about Unexpected Leaders. Do pay attention, because we will end the unit with a test on Friday."

Several kids groaned.

"Here's how this works," Ms. Tottenham continued. "Once you pair up, I'll assign each pair an unexpected leader. You'll have twenty minutes to prepare a short presentation, which you'll give during the second half of class. Got it?"

A sea of nodding heads.

"All right," she said, clapping her hands again. "Find a partner and then I'll assign you a leader. Try to find someone you haven't worked with before, please."

As usual, I felt the pang of Teagan not being there, but

also relief that I didn't have to work with Aaliyah again. We hadn't said a word to each other since the incident in the hallway, which I considered an improvement.

Zuri caught my eye and we partnered up. She looked as grateful as I did that she didn't have to work with Aaliyah.

I gathered my things so Zuri and I could find a spot on the floor to work. In front of me, Aaliyah was twisted in her seat, scanning the classroom.

"Ah, Aaliyah," Ms. Tottenham said, coming over. "Looks like we're an odd number today with Marcus home sick. Why don't you be a trio with Josiah and Victoria?"

"That's okay," Aaliyah said. "I don't mind working by myself."

But as I sat down next to Zuri, I caught a glimpse of Aaliyah's face. It told a different story.

That was the same look Teagan had on Friday in the studio, when she was so upset about Main Line. It was how Isaiah looked last week when I snapped at him in the cafeteria. And it was how I imagined I looked every time I wished Teagan was here beside me.

It was the face of someone who needed a friend.

Zuri and I got to work, but through all the Unexpected Leader presentations, I couldn't get Ernest P. Boyd's words out of my head.

For glorious this world would be
If men stopped burning bridges
And held out their hands instead

The ache in my belly was still coming back every time I thought about how Aaliyah had treated me in the hallway, but each time it ached a little less. And as I spoke to more and more students about why we should make Kelly welcoming for all, I knew for certain her words weren't true. I knew I could be a voice for my classmates, even with my stutter.

I watched Aaliyah standing alone in the front of the classroom, rocking her presentation on Claudette Colvin.

Maybe—just maybe—it was time to hold out my hand.

"I don't think anyone should have to go through that," I said to Isaiah at our lockers after school, once I'd described what happened with Aaliyah and the partners in social studies.

"All the more reason to stick with your platform," Isaiah said.

It was true, and a little absurd—me fighting for change that would benefit my so-called enemy. I chuckled to myself.

"Ready to go?" Isaiah asked, shoving his math book into his backpack. "My mom should be outside in a few minutes to take us to Liberty."

Shoot. I didn't have my math book. I must have left it in Mr. Newton's classroom earlier. I told Isaiah as much, and that I'd meet him outside.

Mr. Newton's classroom was on the other side of the media center, so I started making my way across it. The open area was dotted with students sitting at tables or sprawled on the floor on their stomachs, some working on the media center's tablets, others flipping lazily through library books and jotting down notes.

Oh. No.

Most of these students were eighth graders. I spied the boy who had called me G-G-G-Gabby.

"Hey, Lonely Loser," a voice called out. The kind of voice that sounded friendly on its surface, but boiled with nastiness beneath.

The voice had come from the girl with the magenta-tipped extensions, the same girl who had stopped Aaliyah in the hallway to laugh at her hairstyle. She was sitting cross-legged on the floor and looking right at me. No. Past me.

I whirled around to find Aaliyah standing behind me,

holding a tub of books labeled *Ms. Tottenham's class: To be returned.*

For a moment, Aaliyah and I stood frozen in place, as if we were in a movie and someone had pressed PAUSE. I stared at her. She stared at the girl with the magenta-tipped extensions. And then she began to move again, walking determinedly in the direction of the returns desk, holding tight to her bin of books.

I continued toward Mr. Newton's room, but had only made it past the librarian's desk when—

CRASH.

A library book skittered across the floor, collided with the toe of my sneaker, and stopped.

I spun around. Aaliyah was sprawled across the floor with the scattered books all around her, and the girl with the magenta-tipped extensions was looking down at her own outstretched leg in an elaborate show of shock, as if it had acted all on its own. "Gosh, I'm so sorry. I was just stretching. You should *really* watch where you're going. But kudos on the landing. I'd give you a perfect ten."

I could almost hear Ernest P. Boyd whispering in my ear. *And held out their hands instead.*

My brow furrowed and I rushed forward, grabbing as many books as I could and placing them back in the bin.

Aaliyah had already gotten to her feet. There was dust on the front of her pants, but either she didn't notice or she didn't care. She held out her hands for the bin.

"S-Sorry," I whispered. "Th-That wasn't—She-She sh-shouldn't—" I wanted to say so many things to Aaliyah, all the words came out at once, overlapping one another until I hardly made any sense at all.

"Just give me my stuff!" Aaliyah hissed.

"Hey!" I shot back, louder than I'd meant to. "I-I'm just tr-trying to help you h-here!"

I shoved the yellow bin at her, now halfway refilled with books. She turned away from me to pick up the rest, but not before I got a clear look at her face, at those hazel eyes beneath a set of dark brows. They were filled with tears.

Not Aaliyah Reade-Johnson, who scared even her hair into place. There was no way I had seen that girl about to cry. That was all I could think about as Mrs. Jordan drove us to Liberty and while Isaiah and I killed time waiting for poetry to start. Aaliyah was the only sixth grader I knew who was brave enough to raise her hand and speak her mind, even if other kids rolled their eyes and sucked their teeth when she did it.

And had what I'd done counted as reaching out a hand? Aaliyah didn't seem to think so.

"Okay," Red said that afternoon at poetry, snapping me from my thoughts. Teagan had sat down on one side of me, Isaiah on the other. "Let's start with an exercise today. Isaiah has been reading, well, what *hasn't* he been reading lately?"

We all laughed.

"He was telling me about this poem he read called 'Ode on a Grecian Urn.' I don't really know what was so fly about an urn that the dude felt he needed to write a poem about it, but that seems like a cool idea—writing a poem that addresses someone or something directly. There aren't any rules here—write an ode to the cafeteria tater tots if you want."

"Why would anybody want to do that?" Alejandro tossed out, smiling.

"I would!" Teagan chimed in. "The tater tots at Main Line are *divine*." She dramatically put her hands on her heart, as if fried potatoes made her life complete. I giggled. Teagan seemed more relaxed than she had on Friday, and I was glad.

"Good point, Alejandro," Red said, laughing. "Very good point. Now, let's get vibin' and versin'!"

I thought first about writing a poem to Mrs. Baxter and then one for Ms. Tottenham. But then another idea came to me. It wasn't an ode, exactly, but it was something close. I turned to a new page in my journal.

A little while later, when Red asked if anyone wanted to share, I kept quiet.

I would share this poem, but not here. These words were for one person only: the person who needed to hear them the most.

A Poem for Aaliyah

I know we haven't always seen eye to eye
But I'll tell you what I've seen with mine
A girl who's strong, who's fierce, and true
A brilliant speaker and a natural leader, too
I've seen a girl with confidence, enough to go around
Who can make others stand up straight with just a
 single raised brow
And when she speaks, oh, the world, it stops and listens
For her words reach out and grab you and make you
 pay attention

She's smart, she's brave, this girl named Aaliyah,
just come have a look and see
She'll inspire you to be the same, just like she
inspires me

The next day, I folded up the poem, wrote Aaliyah's name on it, and slipped it into her locker. I didn't know if Mr. Ernest P. Boyd would consider this a bridge built, but it was a start. One brick in what might someday become a bridge.

For Your Eyes Only

Chapter 15

The next couple of days flew by, and before I knew it, it was Thursday and time for our final speech practice in Ms. Tottenham's room. I arrived second this time. Aaliyah was already there, scribbling madly in a notebook resting on her knees. She hadn't so much as glanced at me since I'd slipped the poem in her locker Tuesday morning, but when I entered, she looked up and then quickly snapped her notebook shut. Then she pressed her lips together in what may have been a smile—or maybe she was trying to get the broccoli from today's lunch out of her back teeth. Either way, bridges were built one brick at a time, so I flashed her a quick smile before I took my seat.

This time Ms. Tottenham got started before we'd even finished our lunch. "Time is of the essence, leaders," she declared, and called Layla and Kayla to the podium. Darrin and Dominique followed, and then it was Aaliyah's turn.

I had to admit—everyone had gotten much better. Layla and Kayla said "party" eight times instead of twelve and managed not to giggle even once during their speech. Darrin only slashed the air with his fist a few times, and Dominique managed to say her speech in a normal tone of voice. Still, none of them could compare to Aaliyah. If possible, she'd gone from extraordinary to out of this world. She'd added more lines to her speech that were even more powerful than the ones from before, and her voice didn't falter. Not even once. In the midst of our applause, Darrin muttered, "Man, she makes us *all* look bad."

He was right, of course.

There was no denying that.

My insides clenched just as Ms. Tottenham called, "Gabriela, you're up."

When I'd left Mrs. Baxter's office yesterday, she'd told me that as long as I felt brilliant when reading my speech, I'd be brilliant. I stood at the podium and stared out at my classmates, willing myself to feel brilliant, even though I had to follow Aaliyah, a.k.a. Brilliance Personified.

I took a belly-breath and looked out at my audience,

then let my words and exhale start at the same time. "G-Good afternoon. My name is Gabriela McBride, and I'm running for Sixth-Grade Ambassador, because I want to make K-Kelly Middle School the kind of place where all students feel www-welcome."

I made it through the rest of my speech with only a few more bumps. When it came time for feedback, Kayla and Layla said, in near-perfect unison, "That was totally amazing!" Dominique and Darrin agreed. Ms. Tottenham turned to Aaliyah. My heart skipped a beat.

"I think Gabriela sounded better than last time," Aaliyah said.

"Better how?" Ms. Tottenham prompted.

Aaliyah shrugged. Ms. Tottenham pursed her lips and turned away. "I guess more confident," Aaliyah said, not looking at Ms. Tottenham or at me. Then she shrugged again.

Should I consider that another brick?

I didn't have time to decide—the bell rang before I made it back to my seat. I gathered up my things and headed toward the door, nodding to Aaliyah on my way out, and hoping, hoping that with enough small changes, enough bricks, we'd eventually build a bridge between us.

I trudged into social studies a couple hours later and found my seat. Like she had during the meeting at lunch, Ms. Tottenham got started right away, this time with a slide show about leaders during the women's rights movement.

"No need to take notes just yet," she said.

Aaliyah, who had been writing in her notebook, stopped momentarily. Then, when Ms. Tottenham wasn't looking, she went back to writing like her life depended on it. *She's probably making her speech even better,* I thought, my spirits sagging a bit. I had to admit it—I wouldn't *mind* winning. If I could figure out a way to get through to the seventh and eighth graders, find a way to get them totally on board with my platform . . .

Being a leader is not about winning, I reminded myself just as Aaliyah turned quickly in her chair and dropped a folded square of paper on my desk. She'd written my name in her neat, slanted handwriting, and beneath that, *For your eyes ONLY.*

Heart pounding, I pulled open the folded piece of paper, placed it beneath my desk so no one else but me could see, and began to read.

For Your Eyes Only

Dear Gabriela,

Thank you for the poem, and most of all, thank you for caring enough to write it. I know I owe you an apology for calling you Repeat all this time. So, from the bottom of my heart, I'm sorry. I know I've hurt your feelings a lot, so saying I'm sorry might not mean much to you, and an explanation might not mean much, either, but I'd like to try anyway.

Last year, when I first moved to Philly, I had a hard time making friends. It was the same way in my old school. I know people think I'm bossy and have too many opinions, but that's just me. I don't know how to be any other way. So I made up my mind when my family moved to Philly to stop trying to make friends. But then I noticed you and

Teagan and you two were, well, a little different, too. Not different in a bad way, but just not like everyone else. Teagan with that hat she always wore and that notebook she carried, and you always writing poems all over every page of your notes. I saw you two and I thought you'd accept me and my weirdness, too, even though everyone else wouldn't. And then I asked to sit with you at lunch, and you hesitated. I could see you thinking of a reason to say no. And I guess I had been hoping so much that I would finally have some friends, that it hurt A LOT when you basically said no. So that's why I started making fun of you. You'd hurt me and I wanted to hurt you, too. It's not right, and I know that now. So again, I'm sorry. I hope you can forgive me. And thanks again for the poem. I'm good at writing *speeches, but when you speak from your heart through poetry, your words have a way of making people (or at least me) listen.*

Sincerely,
Aaliyah

P.S. I wonder if you might want to be friends someday, you know, when you've forgiven me?

I didn't know what I was expecting the letter to say, but at least one thing surprised me—that Aaliyah thought my stuttering meant we didn't want her to sit with us. I had never thought about how that moment might have felt for Aaliyah.

When the bell rang signaling the end of class, Aaliyah packed up quickly and made a beeline for the door. I raced to catch up, falling in step beside her.

"Th-Thanks," I said, holding up the letter she'd written me.

"You're welcome." She paused, stopped in her tracks, and turned to face me. "I meant every word of it. I really am sorry."

"I'm ssssorry, too," I said.

Aaliyah frowned. "For what?"

"For ssssnapping at y-you outside the library that d-day with the b-books and for m-making you fffeel un-unwelcome at my l-lunch t-table last year."

Aaliyah smiled at me, such a wide, bright, rivaling-the-sunshine smile, I didn't have to wonder if she was trying to remove broccoli from her back teeth.

"You're not going to believe this," I said to Teagan as soon as she dropped her boulder backpack along the wall of studio six on Friday. I told her everything, from Isaiah sending me the poem to the incident in the library, from me writing Aaliyah the poem, to the letter I'd received today.

"Wow. Just wow, Gabby," she said when I was done, shaking her head and laughing a little. "Even if you don't win the election—just think about it: You've already built a bridge right there."

Ernest P. Boyd would be proud.

"I mean it," Teagan continued. "I was worried about you and Aaliyah, but I've been impressed. You're going to be just fine at Kelly without me."

I nodded. I already was.

"All right, people!" Red clapped his hands as usual. "I've got a special project for us today—a group piece. The theme is change."

Nice! We hadn't done a group piece since we performed at Rhythm and Views when Liberty reopened this summer. I loved how everyone's different voices wove together to form one message.

"What kind of change?" Teagan asked. "There's change like nickels and quarters, or change like what Gabby's trying to do at Kelly, or change like delta in math, which means—"

"Teagan," I said. "Your Main Line is showing."

We all laughed.

"There's changing, like growing," Isaiah added. "And changes, um . . . we go through changes when we mature from, um, kids to teenagers, if you know what I mean." He blushed.

"Oh, I know what you mean!" Alejandro said, his voice cracking on the last word as if on cue.

This time I laughed so hard tears filled my eyes.

"It's all good, poets! All good!" Red said as the laughter died down. "But how about we start with this: a change in perspective. Take a few seconds and think of a time you changed your view on something. When you've got something, let's just start calling things out."

The first thing that popped into my head, of course, was this year with Aaliyah. We'd gone from enemies to . . . something like friends.

"I think I'm actually starting to like Shakespeare," Alejandro said after a few moments of silence, "thanks to getting to know this bro right here." He tipped his chin toward Isaiah.

Bria chimed in. "I used to complain all the time, but then my grandma taught me to say three things I'm grateful for each night before bed. You should thank her for that—I'm much more fun to be around now."

That got another laugh from the group.

As we threw out more ideas, a rush of warmth washed over me. Everyone was sharing such wonderful—and different—things, and we couldn't get enough of it, couldn't get enough of each other. That was the magic of this group. It was why on some Mondays and Fridays, I couldn't get out of Kelly and into poetry fast enough. In here, we weren't sixth or seventh graders or the Shakespeare kid or the girl who stutters. We were poets, doing what we loved together and getting to know each other in the process until our differences didn't matter at all. We did a lot of laughing in studio six, but we never laughed *at* each other, only ever *with* each other.

Imagine, I thought to myself, *if Kelly could be like this.*

Hold up. What if I could help *make* Kelly be like this?

Because they were seventh graders, I never would have gotten to know Alejandro and Bria if we didn't have this poetry group. Alejandro would never have known he liked Shakespeare if it weren't for Isaiah.

It was the doing something together that brought us closer together. What if, instead of just getting rid of Sixth-Grade Initiation, I replaced it with something else—something where sixth, seventh, and eighth graders could work together?

I knew that Ernest P. Boyd would definitely consider that a bridge built.

By the time I got to hip-hop, I was so full of energy, I thought my feet might punch holes through Liberty's ancient hardwood floors.

Now *this* was an unbeatable platform.

Changes
By the Liberty Poets

Change is the least predictable thing.
Sometimes it attacks,

Like soldiers ambushing an enemy.
Sometimes it's sneaky,
Like grandma's hair going gray.
Sometimes it's just what you need,
A challenge, ready to be conquered.
And sometimes it's the last thing you want,
A turnover that allows the game-winning point . . . for the other team.
Sometimes it's easier said than done,
Like downing a mouthful of school tater tots.
And sometimes, it's not as hard as you believe,
Like crossing a raging river, once you've discovered a bridge.
"Can't you make up your mind?" we ask.
"Don't you see?" Change replies. "That's the point."
"Without changing of minds there can be no change.
And that is how history's made."

Pink Tutus

Chapter 16

Before I knew it, it was election day. I woke up to a text from Teagan: *All fingers and toes crossed for you today! And remember, if you get nervous, imagine the whole audience in leotards and pink tutus.*

I burst out laughing at the thought of Josiah and Marcus in frilly pink tutus. My nerves settled down a bit, but by second period, the Tiny Tot tappers were back in my belly.

The election assembly was scheduled to take place during fourth period, just before sixth-grade lunch.

"That's probably so no one gets onstage and throws up," a boy whispered to another in my first-period class.

He was probably right.

By the middle of third period, my insides were doing backflips and my nerves were sending electric shocks through my whole body, right down to the tips of my toes.

"All students running for ambassador please report to room 127. Again, all students running for ambassador please report to room 127."

I got numbly to my feet and made my way to the classroom door. Voices went off like fireworks.

"Good luck, Gabby!"

"Knock 'em dead!"

I waved my thanks, then made it in a haze to Ms. Tottenham's room. The air inside buzzed with the steady white noise of excited voices. No one was more excited than the twins, Kayla and Layla, who punctuated almost every other sentence with a squeal. Aaliyah sat in her usual seat, her head bent over her speech.

"Backpack in the corner, Gabriela," Ms. Tottenham called to me.

Mutely, I dropped my backpack on the pile with the rest and made my way over to my usual seat, my speech in hand. I'd revised my speech after last Friday's poetry meeting, but I'd made some more small—okay, big—changes last night. She didn't know this, but Aaliyah had inspired them.

"Hey, Gabriela," Aaliyah said, glancing up to look at me. She wore her usual bun and a suit. An actual suit, with a button-up jacket and a knee-length black skirt.

She squinted at me. "You look a little sweaty."

I wiped nervously at my brow, trying hard not to imagine six hundred sets of eyes, all on me. At the same time.

"Gabriela, do you have a moment?"

I whirled around and saw Mrs. Baxter standing in the doorway and remembered the first time she had picked me up for a session this school year. Aaliyah had whispered, *Have fun at speech, Repeat*. I glanced at her now. Something on her face told me that she remembered that, too. She caught my eye and smiled just as Mrs. Baxter placed a hand on either of my shoulders.

"Good luck today, Gabby," she said, looking right into my eyes. "Remember to speak on the breath and use your rhythm." Then she pressed something into my hand, a folded index card. "Just a little something to remind you to be brave."

On the card was the Saint Francis of Assisi quote, written in Mrs. Baxter's loopy handwriting: *Start by doing what's necessary; then do what's possible; and suddenly you are doing the impossible.*

She squeezed my shoulder, wished me luck once more, and left. I tucked the index card into my pocket and started back to my seat, but only made it halfway before a frazzled Ms. Tottenham said, "It's time. We need to get to the auditorium—now."

She hustled us toward the door, and me away from my

speech, still lying on my desk. "B-But m-my—" Before I could get my words out, Aaliyah appeared beside me, holding my speech.

"Th-Thanks."

We spilled out into the hallway, Kayla and Layla on our heels.

"What's on your note card?" Aaliyah asked.

I pulled the card out and showed her, just as Layla said, "Aaliyah, you look like the lady who does our mom's taxes."

Kayla giggled.

All at once, I was back in the hallway when that stupid boy made fun of Isaiah and I couldn't find my words. Whether I won the election or not, I knew I would never fail to stand up for a friend again. I stopped walking and turned to face the twins. "I-I think-think A-Aaliyah looks very . . . pro-professional!" I said, a little louder than I'd intended.

Kayla and Layla stared at me, almost-identical looks of shock upon their almost-identical faces.

"Thank you, Gabriela," Aaliyah said. We turned and walked confidently toward the auditorium, leaving a stunned and silent Kayla and Layla in our wake. My words may have been bumpy, but I'd just proven that I could stand up and make people listen when I spoke.

"Are you ready to do what seems impossible?" Aaliyah asked as we approached the auditorium.

I nodded, my heart a bass drum in my chest. I was.

Every single sixth, seventh, and eighth grader was in the auditorium, and every single teacher, too. I scanned the crowd, looking for a familiar face. Isaiah sat off to the right with his fourth-period class. He caught my eye and pumped his fist in the air as Ms. Tottenham ushered the six of us past the seventh- and eighth-grade candidates to a line of empty seats right smack in the middle of the front row. Each seat had a piece of paper taped to it that read *Reserved*.

"Ooooh, it's like we're stars at the Grammys!" Kayla squealed. Then she proceeded to wave to the crowd and blow kisses until Ms. Tottenham gently asked her to take a seat.

I sat down beside Aaliyah and turned around to take in the crowd again. It was bigger than the one at Liberty's Rhythm and Views show this past summer. I wiped my sweaty palms on my jeans. *Start by doing what's necessary; then do what's possible; and suddenly you are doing the impossible.*

"Okay," Ms. Tottenham said, crouching down to address the six of us. She held a small stack of programs in one hand and a cordless mic in the other. "I'm going to go onstage and say a few words about the Kelly Ambassadors. Then we'll get right into speeches, starting with you six." Ms. Tottenham paused to hand each of us a program. "Make note of the order. Darrin, you're up first, followed by Layla and Kayla. Then Dominique, Gabby, and Aaliyah—you're our final sixth-grade speaker. Got it?"

"Got it," said Aaliyah.

The rest of us bobbed our heads in silence. Now that the assembly was about to begin, even the twins looked subdued, wearing similar looks of panic mixed with shock, as though they suddenly had no idea how they'd gotten there or what they were about to do.

So many times in my life already I had sat in an auditorium, waiting for my turn on the stage. But this time was different. This time I wasn't going onstage to perform or entertain through dance. I'd be using only my voice, my words. The last time I'd done that, I'd recited a poem with almost all of my Liberty family onstage behind me. But today? It was just me. Just my voice, and my words. Would they be strong enough alone?

They had to be.

Ms. Tottenham walked onto the stage, clutching her cordless mic. Applause broke out immediately, with more than a few of the seventh and eighth graders calling out, "That's my favorite teacher!" and, "Ms. T is the best!"

Ms. Tottenham smiled, waiting patiently for the excitement to die down. When at last the auditorium was silent, she said, "Good morning, Kelly scholars, esteemed educators, and parents, guardians, and family. Welcome to the eighth annual Kelly Ambassadors Election Assembly."

At once another great swell of applause erupted, accompanied by whistles and yells. It took Ms. Tottenham a few minutes more to make it through her short speech. She ended it with a laugh and said, "Kelly enthusiasm is second to none. And now, without further delay, I'd like to introduce our first candidate, sixth grader Darrin Gibbs."

There was another round of applause and a brief chant of "Darrin, Darrin, Darrin" from the football players scattered throughout the audience until Ms. Tottenham stood and pressed her fingers to her lips.

Darrin cleared his throat and began his speech, his fist slashing through the air as he read. Even though he was talking about double-portion-sized lunches, he said his words with so much conviction, by the time he finished, I found myself wondering if I'd been cheated all these years by only being served one sandwich instead of two.

The twins followed Darrin, and delivered their speech

about Kelly's social life—or lack thereof—without so much as a falter or slip of the tongue. Not even a single giggle or squeal. Everyone was so good, even better than they'd been at the final practice run. They sounded so confident, so professional.

After the applause for the twins died down, Dominique took the stage. I knew each second she spoke into the microphone was one second closer to my turn to do the same.

My heart began to race again. I took a deep breath and then another. Aaliyah leaned over and whispered, "You'll be fine, Gabby." Then she squeezed my arm, kind of like how Teagan squeezed my hand whenever she knew I needed an extra boost of confidence. Grateful, I whispered, "Thank you," then turned my attention back to the stage.

"So vote for me for Sixth-Grade Ambassador if you want to expand our intramural programs to include all the sports we love," Dominique concluded. Then she raised both fists in the air. The audience cheered, none more loudly than Dominique's double Dutch team.

"Thank you, Dominique," Ms. Tottenham said, taking center stage again. "And now for our penultimate sixth-grade speaker, Gabriela McBride."

Propelled by applause and a "Let's go, cuz!" from

Red, I made my way up the stairs, my speech shaking in my hand.

"Make sure to stand close enough to the mic," Ms. Tottenham whispered gently. "And best of luck." And then she was gone, on her way back to her seat, leaving me in the middle of the stage with nothing but a crumpled piece of loose-leaf paper and more than one thousand eyes on me.

Everyone Welcome

Chapter 17

"G-Good m-morning. My-My n-name is Gabriela McBride, a-and and th-though I may be running for Sixth-Grade Ambass-Ambassador, I'm here to be the v-voice of each and every sssssingle one of you, re-re-regardless of your grade. I'm running because I want to make K-Kelly Middle School the kind of place where all st-students feel www-welcome. Sixth graders, how many of you got hit with water balloons on the first day of school?"

Just like I'd imagined, pretty much all the sixth-grade hands went up.

"Ssssixth, seventh, and eighth-eighth graders—how many people felt unwelcome when those n-n-nicknames were put on the lockers, either this year or the year you first started at K-Kelly?"

Once again, most of the sixth-grade hands went up, but this time some seventh- and eighth-grade hands joined in. My eyes found Isaiah, who sat on the edge of his seat, looking back at me with an encouraging smile on his face.

So far, so good.

"You know from my flyers I want to get rid of Sixth-Grade Initiation—"

"Yeah, what's that about?" a boy shouted from somewhere in the eighth-grade section. "Traditions are traditions. You can't just—" A teacher shushed him before he could say anything else.

I took a deep breath.

"Well, I'd like to get rid of Sixth-Grade Initiation and rrrr-replace it with something even better. I imagine an all-day event where seventh and eighth graders host challenges for sixth graders—including a water balloon challenge—"

That got some whoops from the audience. I had their attention now.

"But I don't want to st-stop there. Mmmm-Making Kelly welcoming and fun for everyone ssshhh-shouldn't be a once-a-year thing. There should be more events throughout the year that sixth, sssseventh, and eighth graders can do t-t-together. Because everyone brings something different to this school, and the mmm-more we get to know each other, the mmm-more those differences be-become not ssssomething to call out or make fun of, but something to celebrate."

I found Aaliyah in the crowd, looked right at her, and continued.

"And speaking of differences, you may have noticed I-I'm not-not really all that g-good with sp-speeches. S-So I thought I'd try something d-different instead."

Last night, after I'd practiced my speech for the millionth time, I'd read Aaliyah's letter again, and her words about how I had a talent for speaking from my heart through poetry gave me an idea. I had pulled out the mint-green flyer. Nope. It didn't say anywhere I couldn't do a poem for my speech.

A shout came from the audience. "Good on you, my lady!"

Isaiah. He must have figured out by now what I was up to. *This is for you, Fakespeare,* I thought.

The audience laughed, and the glacier inside me melted. I took in the sea of faces before me, including Red, Isaiah, Bria, Alejandro. Aaliyah and Ms. Tottenham. I thought of the way Kelly looked to me on that first day—exciting, but big and scary, too. The way it felt when I thought I wasn't welcome, and the way it must have felt for kids who still believed they weren't. I thought about all of that and began to speak, quiet and hesitant at first, louder and with more conviction as I went on.

"There s-sits a place on K-Kelly Dr-Drive
An or-or-ordinary b-building
Colossal in its size
The wwwalls themselves hold nothing
Neither promise nor demise
Until twelve hundred st-students
Excited
Scared
Make their way inside

The old and new together
Best friends and frenemies
That one quirky
That one bold
That one with star-shaped cheese."

I chanced another look out at Isaiah when a few people laughed. He was beaming. With another deep breath, I continued.

"It's then we make a choice
About how we live this year
Do we stand together?
Or do we tease
Taunt
Jeer?

Imagine if we changed all that
Flung doors all open wide
Beckoned to each and every kid:
'Come in.
You're welcome inside.'

Oh, Kelly, let's begin
To fix the ties that broke
Let's start anew and clear the air
Of bullies
Boos
And jokes
Let's instead reach out our hands
Build bridges in between
Let's listen to all voices
Let everyone be seen

Quirky
Bold
Excited
Scared
Frenemies into friends
That's my dream, all laid out
It's how I hope this ends

If you agree
Stand with me—
Check the box next to Gabby McBride
And together
Tomorrow
We'll do this thing—
We'll welcome everyone inside."

The sparks were flying off my words, I could tell, but as soon as I finished . . .

Silence.

Heat rose in my face. Maybe it was a mistake to do the poem. Now I just looked foolish. Now I—

The applause was sudden. And thunderous. Isaiah was on his feet. Then Red, Alejandro, and Bria. Aaliyah, too. A few more people stood, and then a few more until there were just as many people standing as sitting.

Ms. Tottenham came to stand beside me. "I knew you could do it," she said to me, shouting over the sounds of clapping and cheering.

With a smile so big I thought it would break my face, I found my way back down the stairs and to my seat.

"Great job," Aaliyah whispered as the audience quieted down. "That was amazing."

"And now for our final sixth-grade speaker, Aaliyah Reade-Johnson."

I gave Aaliyah's arm a quick squeeze as she got up and walked toward the stage, empty-handed. She stood before the mic and looked right out at the audience. Then she began her speech from memory, just as she had in Ms. Tottenham's classroom. Her voice rang out, flawless and smooth, each word a call to action. All around the auditorium, people were nodding in agreement with what Aaliyah had to say, and by the time she finished, almost the whole auditorium was on their feet.

She returned to her seat, breathless and smiling.

"That was awesome," I whispered to her as Ms. Tottenham took to the stage to introduce the seventh-grade speakers.

Aaliyah beamed at me.

I didn't know if either of us would win in the end, but we were friends now. And that made both of us victorious.

Two in the Place of One

Chapter 18

The rest of the day flew by in a blur. That afternoon Ms. Tottenham handed out paper ballots to everyone in social studies. We checked off our choices for the three grades' ambassadors and then handed the ballots back.

"Results will be tallied sometime tomorrow afternoon, at which point I will personally notify each winner," Ms. Tottenham called as we packed up for the end of the day.

Mama, Daddy, Red, and I met up for ice cream that night with Teagan and Mr. Harmon to celebrate my speech.

"Heard you knocked their socks off," Mr. Harmon said, grinning wide beneath his bushy gray mustache.

"You know it, Mr. Harmon," Red replied, piling his spoon high with a mess of chocolate ice cream covered with chocolate syrup and sprinkles.

"I wish I could've been there," Teagan said, disappointment in her voice.

"Us, too," Mama said. Neither she nor Daddy could make it to the assembly today. "But not to worry." She pulled out her phone. "A certain speech therapist who was extremely proud of her student may have sent me some video."

"Mama, come on," I said, my face growing hot. But Mama had already hit PLAY and held it up so everyone could see. I covered my face as my voice erupted from the phone.

"Awesome sauce!" Teagan declared. "I told you it would be a piece of cake." She pretended to brush her shoulders off.

"Hey, that's my move!" Red cried. Chocolate ice cream exploded from his mouth and dribbled down the front of his shirt.

Teagan and I laughed until I thought my face and heart would burst.

The next morning, I sat in my first-period language arts class, trying as hard as I could to focus on the questions my teacher was asking about *The Giver.* But all I could think about was the result of the election. Three more periods until lunch, and then it was officially afternoon, right?

By math class, I still hadn't heard from Ms. Tottenham. I wondered if that meant I hadn't won.

But maybe Aaliyah had. My spirits lifted a little at the thought. When the bell rang, I ran to social studies to find out.

"Have you heard yet?"

Aaliyah shook her head.

"Do you know if anyone else has—?"

She shook her head again, so hard I thought her bun might come loose. And then I remembered who I was talking to. I chuckled to myself.

I plopped down in my chair and tried to concentrate as Ms. Tottenham continued our unit on Leaders in Women's History. Once, when she was talking about how suffragist Carrie Chapman Catt had been elected president of the National American Woman Suffrage Association, I thought she winked at me, but it could have just as easily been Aaliyah.

Remember, I reminded myself. *If your platform got through to just one person, you're already a winner.*

It turned out that that one person—who I hoped was actually just one of many—sat to the left of me. We were partnering up and I tapped Aaliyah on the shoulder just as Zuri asked if she wanted to be her partner. After an awkward moment, I said I'd work with Josiah, who must have thought I was crazy, I was smiling so big.

My nerves calmed a bit as we worked. That is, until Ms. Tottenham called me and Aaliyah up to her desk. We shared a look.

The Tiny Tots were tapping in my belly again. This was it.

"Well, Gabriela, Aaliyah," Ms. Tottenham said once she'd sat down behind her desk. She looked back and forth between us. "Something unusual happened. Something that's only ever happened once before."

I did a sideways glance toward Aaliyah. She shrugged.

Ms. Tottenham continued. "We tallied the votes for Sixth-Grade Ambassador and . . . you two were tied for first place. You should both be proud!"

The Tiny Tots lost it in my belly, like when Mama let them "free dance" and they banged the floor as hard and as fast as they could. I'd actually gotten as many votes as Aaliyah Reade-Johnson. How was *that* for unexpected?

"Normally, in this situation, it's Kelly Ambassador policy to have the two of you write and deliver new speeches and have the student body vote again. That would happen next week." She paused. "Are you both prepared to do that?"

I blinked. A whole other speech. For a brief moment, I considered conceding to Aaliyah—I'd already seen my platform at work, after all. But I'd come so far. I imagined the change I could make as ambassador—ideas for more mixed-grade events were already swirling around in my brain. I didn't want to give that up.

But I didn't want Aaliyah to have to give that up, either.

I looked over at Aaliyah. Her face was hard to read, but that was nothing new. It was different somehow, though. Shy, I realized. She turned to me.

"Gabby," she said, her eyes glancing from the floor up to me and then back down again. "I liked what you had to say about building a community, and I'd like to see that happen, too, so . . . I was thinking, if it's okay with Ms. Tottenham, that maybe we could just, um, share the role and be Sixth-Grade Ambassadors together?"

I didn't so much as pause or hesitate. "I think I'd like that very much."

"Excellent!" Ms. Tottenham said. "That's an even better idea than a runoff election. I think you two will be perfect together, two natural leaders."

A warm rush of pride engulfed me at the sound of being called a natural leader like Aaliyah.

Two in the Place of One

The next day, Isaiah was just opening his lunchbox when Aaliyah approached our table.

"Can I sit with you?"

For the second time in two days, I didn't hesitate.

"Of course."

After she took out a composition notebook, she followed my gaze to the front, where she'd written both of our names with the words *Sixth-Grade Ambassadors* beneath them.

"Who would've thought you two would be sitting here like this together now," Isaiah said, looking from Aaliyah to me and back again. "Guess my parents were right after all: This year should be about branching out."

"Branching out?" Aaliyah asked.

"Yeah, like making changes," Isaiah replied, plucking a tater tot from his tray and shoving it in his mouth. Immediately, he made a face like he'd just tasted battery acid. "Though there are some things I'd like to change back, like bringing lunch from home again."

Aaliyah and I laughed, as I began to think about all the changes that had happened that school year so far. I'd started sixth grade without my best friend, and was now giggling at lunch with my mortal enemy. And now the two of us were going to work together to change Kelly for the better, for everyone.

"Anything you'd like to change back if you could?" Isaiah asked, poking at a slightly singed chicken nugget with his fork.

I glanced across the table at Aaliyah, who had already turned to a blank page in the notebook and written *Community Building Action Plan.*

"No," I said, grinning. "I wouldn't change a thing."

About the Author

Teresa E. Harris earned her bachelor's degree in English from Columbia University and an MFA in Writing for Children from Vermont College, where she won numerous awards, including the Flying Pig Grade-A, Number-One Ham Humor Award. She is a high school English teacher in New Jersey, where she lives with three very bossy cats. She spends most of her time grading papers and writing novels, and though she was never an ambassador like Gabby when she was in sixth grade, Teresa was the president of her high school's National Honor Society.

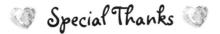

Special Thanks

With gratitude to **Leana Barbosa**, M.S. CCC-SLP, for contributing her knowledge of speech therapies and language pathology; to **Fatima Goss Graves**, Senior Vice President for Program, National Women's Law Center, for her insights into the experiences and perspectives of modern African American children; and **Sofia Snow**, program director at Urban Word NYC, for guiding Gabriela's poetic journey.

American Girl would also like to give a special shout-out to **Urban Word NYC First Draft Open Mic** for inspiring the "First draft!" tradition for Gabriela's poetry group in this book.

READY FOR ANOTHER CURTAIN CALL?

Visit

americangirl.com

to learn more about Gabriela's world!